The Crystals of Gorn

Bringing Light to the Darkness

By
Tony Peter

PUBLISH AMERICA

PublishAmerica
Baltimore

ISBN: 978-1-4489-2734-0 (softcover)
ISBN: 978-1-4489-8876-1 (hardcover)
PUBLISHED BY PUBLISHAMERICA, LLLP
www.publishamerica.com
Baltimore

Printed in the United States of America

This book is dedicated to the memory of my late parents, Joe and Josie Peter, who encouraged me to pursuit my dreams and supported me in achieving a life-long career in teaching and caring for youth.

I wish to acknowledge the support I have received in writing this story and to say thank you to my wife and best friend, Betty, and to each of my children, Kristie, Lyla and Bruce. Without your encouragement I would have left this story in its infant form and never followed up on a short story prepared for a middle year class. Thanks also goes to Mary Kowalyshyn, a teacher colleague, who challenged me to write a short story for her class and from which came the inspiration for the Crystals of Gorn. Most of all, I thank my Lord for all the blessings I have received and the opportunity to tell the story of two young people facing a dark foe.

The Crystals of Gorn

Bringing Light to the Darkness

-1-

It was a beautiful summer day with the sun shining brightly in a sky across which floated a few fluffy cumulus clouds, like clipper ships plying the seas of old. The wind was slight, barely a kiss upon the cheek, bringing with it the perfume of the many wild flowers that had turned their faces to the sun and released their fragrances. The air was alive with the hum of insects busly gathering nectar and the symphony of song produced by the birds enjoying the warmth of the day. It was a perfect day for the circus to come to town. Suzy was skipping up the hill that overlooked the fair grounds outside of town. She knew from that vantage point she would be able to survey the setting up of the Greatest Show on Earth. She felt her heart begin to race and her breath begin to quicken as she neared the crest of the hill.

From the top of this hill, she could look down on the hustle and bustle of the workers. Large trailers were being unloaded and the elephant had been recruited to place the large mast for the big tent in the hole that had been dug for it. Smaller tents and concession stands were assembled by the hands of the workers as they went about their chore of putting the circus together. Trainers led the many animals around for an exercise walk to limber up the muscles that had become cramped from the trip. Suzy took it all in, her eyes filled with wonder and wishful dreams. She looked over the scene before her as a queen looks over the crowd that gathers outside her residence on such auspicious moments as her birthday or the anniversary of her coronation.

Suzy looked about and found a large rock that had a flat front edge, which overlooked the circus. She moved around in front of the boulder and carefully sat down, with her back to that monolith, while watching for little crawly things. Now she had her throne and could survey her realm as it spread out before her, awaiting a command. The stone had gathered a great deal of heat before her arrival and that added to the comfort of her resting place. Soon, she felt her eyelids growing heavy.

She thought she noticed someone waving to her from the edge of the circus. She squinted and shook her head to clear away the lethargy that had swept over her in those moments of relaxation. She stood up, finding her legs tingling as though they had been asleep for some time. She looked again and saw a figure dressed in black beckoning to her. Without another thought, she began to walk down the hill, drawn by some invisible force, like the needle of a compass to the north magnetic pole.

The figure beckoned once more, turned and shuffled away, her black skirt sweeping the trampled grass. Suzy watched the figure turn at the entrance of a multi-coloured tent to see if she were following. Then she disappeared within. Suzy made her way between the workers who seemed oblivious to her presence. Somewhere in her subconscious mind, it occurred to her that though there was a lot of activity about her she did not hear any sound. Her conscious being, however, did not attach any significance to this and kept her bent on one purpose—to follow the figure that had reached out to her because there seemed to be more to the call than just an idle circus act.

At the entrance, she noticed the threshold of the tent was adorned with strange symbols as well as stylized stars and moons. From within she heard a soft voice calling her by name and inviting her to enter without fear. It did not cross her mind that she should be afraid; the warnings she had received many times at home and at school about strangers were now being ignored. Suzy drew aside the flap of the tent and stepped inside.

Suzy stood still for some time to allow her eyes to adjust to the murk within the enclosure. Slowly her surroundings began to take form and she became aware of a table in the centre of the room, lit by an orb, which glowed with a very light blue radiance. She moved cautiously forward and began to make out the presence of a figure standing behind the glowing sphere. The figure stirred and raised her head revealing a kindly, aged face.

"Come here, my dear. Please do not be afraid. I saw you, my little princess, sitting up on your throne. I have been waiting for you so that I can carry out the task for which I have been born," the lady in black whispered.

Suzy hesitated for a moment, wondering at the reference to her throne—that flat black rock which she had often used to look over the lower levels of her neighbourhood. Then, she let any questions vanish as she looked into those kindly, alluring eyes and moved forward to the empty chair that had suddenly become visible within the gloom of that place. As she slipped around the chair to seat herself, she noticed the large claw-like armrests and the soft purple velvet cushions. Without a second thought, she sat down into the chair. It moulded itself around her and she was aware of the warmth that it emanated, as though someone had just recently abandoned his or her seat of luxury in deference to her.

Suzy began to feel the presence of the lady in black and raised her eyes to meet those large pools of mystery gazing at her with a sense of wonder and caring. The lady smiled slightly as she moved into the large armchair opposite to Suzy, which was identical to the one in which Suzy reposed, except that it was adorned with red velvet.

"Please make yourself very comfortable, little princess, for you will be going on a journey with me to introduce you to the wonders for which you were born and over which you are destined to have immense power and effect. Do not be afraid, especially during a fall, because if you do not give in to the fear you will overcome it and grow stronger from it. Reach out to me if you are alone and I will be there to help you through," the mystery lady calmly explained. "I want you to gaze into the ball in front of you and allow all other thoughts to leave your mind."

Suzy looked at the ball and then looked towards the door, exhibiting some apprehension as what to do next. The lady smiled. "You indeed are correct to be skeptical and wary. I have been very impolite in not introducing myself before now. I am Emeralda, a Sage from a wonderful land near here, and I have come to act as a companion as you embark on an amazing journey."

As the lady smiled Suzy felt relieved and began to peer into the orb before her; suddenly her mind was filled with pictures of her kitchen at home, with her mother working on some pies at the kitchen table assisted by her father who was peeling the fruit for the filling. Her mother raised her head and looked around. Her father stopped and looked at her for a moment before asking, "Are you okay?" Her mother shrugged her shoulders and returned to her work with a slight reply, "It's nothing. Just a feeling like something from long ago."

"Clear your mind, little princess," she heard Emeralda murmuring and Suzy again focused on the ball before her. Instantly, she found herself in the small classroom where she had attended school for the entire seven grades she had completed. She was looking at the set of geometric tools that were hanging from little hooks under the chalkboard. She saw the two set squares and the protractor. Off to the one side were the compass and the divider."

"Concentrate, sweet one. A journey awaits you," pleaded her companion, with a bit more firmness. Suzy struggled to concentrate on the ball before her before she felt her mind slip away to the basement of the little church where weekly Sunday School was held. She found herself looking at the little books that served as curriculum and then she looked across at the Bible, which sat below a picture of the Saviour.

"Pay attention and rid your mind of all these distractions!" came a voice edged with irritation, which left no doubt that this was a command. Suzy snapped to attention and dared not look at Emeralda who, no doubt, would be scowling and sending daggers through her. She fixed her eyes on the ball in front of her and willed herself to direct all her feelings and thoughts toward that orb. Slowly, the ball began to glow and within an orange fog began to swirl. As Suzy focused her entire strength towards the fog it began to clear and she saw before her a star lit sky over a darkened forest. Then, without warning Suzy felt she was hurling towards the forest floor and a scream rose in her throat. She clamped her lips together before the cry could escape from her mouth as she remembered the advice given by the lady in black. The floor rose up to meet her and she almost panicked into screaming. Suddenly, she felt a calm spread over her and very slowly, she landed on the soft forest floor.

Suzy lay very still for just a moment, wondering if any bones were broken, and then she sat up quickly. She looked about carefully and tentatively, aware that something very mysterious had just happened to her. The forest floor was covered with a thick reddish-green moss, which had sunk at least five or six inches where she fallen. She thought the moss had broken her fall and protected her from serious injury. Yet, something told her that was not the case. Suzy saw she had landed in a clearing above which the sky was bright blue. She puzzled briefly since she had earlier seen stars but she let it go. Around the clearing she saw blooming shrubs and within the moss an array of flowers. Suzy peered around at the flowers, which seemed to turn their blossoms towards her. The red, blue and yellow petals appeared to wave at her and presently she became aware of the fragrance of lilac, rose and marigold, subtlety mixed so as not to be overbearing yet poignant enough to be noticed among the many other scents. The trees, with their gnarled and knotted trunks rose toward the sky where the large branches reached out and formed a canopy of thick leaves of an emerald hue. This young girl noticed that the forest was absolutely silent, a fact that she found most unusual since the many groves through which she had previously walked were always alive with the melody of birds and the whispering of the wind in the leaves. As she pondered this lack of sound, she became aware of the soft footfall and rustling of a long skirt. She knew before she saw Emeralda who it was.

"Quickly, little one, get up. We do not have a moment to spare. We must leave here at once or…" Emeralda stopped in mid sentence and Suzy easily added the rest in her mind, 'it will be too late.' The lady peered into Suzy's eyes, then looked away at her hands which she clasped before adding, "or we will miss the show that is waiting for us." She smiled and reached out her hand for Suzy.

Soon, Suzy and the Sage were walking down a winding path that led them out of the deep moss forest. They entered a glade lit by sunbeams filtering through the large leaves and branches, which formed a roof over the opening. Suzy looked around and took in the peaceful calm and beauty of the place. She glanced over at her escort and found that Emeralda was intently staring at a large oak tree on the other side of the glade. She noticed for the first time that the lady wore an earring—no, an emerald stud.

Emeralda must have sensed that her junior companion was studying her because she turned and smiled.

"Let's be on our way. We will cross this opening and pass that oak tree. Beyond is another path that will lead us into a grove of the most unusual trees. Its what all little children dream about." She took Suzy's hand and quickly made her way to the oak tree. Suzy noticed that the tree was very large, old and gnarled, with bunches of acorns in the higher branches. Wrapped around the main trunk and extending along some of the lower branches was a shrub-like growth, which had pale yellowish-green leaves and rather nondescript flowers. Emeralda stopped and pointed to the plant.

"That, my little princess, is the mistletoe. See how this love plant actually lives off the mighty oak, like a leach, a parasite. See the little berries, shining like pearls. Many people are like that plant. They hang on, cling to another, and slowly sap the strength of their host, in the name of love." Emeralda's face contorted as she spoke. "Bah! Just be careful, sweet one."

As they moved on Suzy felt a cold chill and she shuddered. Emeralda's little rant had frightened her and she wondered whether she was wise by following her. The thought soon slipped away as she marveled at the beautiful scenes through which they walked. Suzy blinked her eyes as she gazed ahead. She could not believe the sight that spread out before her. She closed her eyes and pinched herself, willing herself to wake-up. She opened her eyes once again and found that the scene was the same as it had been.

Tall slender crimson-barked trees rose from the forest floor directly ahead of her. The trees were a sight by themselves but what astounded her were the leaves. They were rectangular and she found it hard to believe what they looked like. She moved slowly ahead leaving the lady behind, her eyes never shifting from the fluttering leaves. She now had a close-up look and she observed she had been correct. The leaves were money—bank notes of every denomination and colour and origin. 'Oh!' she thought, 'Wouldn't it be nice to have such a tree.' She sensed that the trees were murmuring to her and she listened carefully to the melodious sounds that they were making. 'Oh yes, I can make them out.' "Come forward, little girl. Reach out and pluck as much as you like. Think of all the things you have ever wanted. Now you can have them all. Just reach out and take all you like. Make your dreams come true." The trees bowed down and Suzy reached out as the trees lured her on.

Suddenly she stopped as she listened to the word 'dream' echo through her mind. Yes, this was only a dream. Money doesn't grow on trees. Mom and dad have often told me that. You have to work to get what you want.

The trees snapped upright taking the money to the highest levels. They were silent and the bark slowly changed its color to a repulsive light green. Suzy felt Emeralda's hand take hers.

"Well done, little one. For a moment, it looked as though you were going to fulfill the dream of every youngster. I now know I was right to bring you along on this adventure."

Soon the two travelers found themselves on the edge of the forest, blinded by the bright sunlight of the midday. They were high above a flat plain on which the cultivated fields alternated with those that were sown with a crop of white flowers. It looked like some vast checkerboard. Far off in the distance Suzy could see the towers of a castle rise above the plain. High up on those towers banners and flags fluttered in the breeze. Suzy stood spellbound as she imagined riding in a coach laden with precious metals and gems pulled by six beautiful horses all decked out with flowers and garlands. The coach was pulling up to the castle and the heralds were announcing its arrival with a trumpet blast.

"Yes, my child, it can all be yours, just as you see it in your vision," Emeralda murmured. "Don't be afraid now for a friend approaches." Suzy looked about and saw an old man with a staff in his hand. He was wearing a tall pointed hat, which was embroidered with stars, bells and planets. He lifted his hand in greeting to the Sage.

"So, Emeralda, you have returned—and with a young one. What is the purpose of this visit?" the old man queried.

The lady chuckled. "Always straight to the point, Marlen. Things haven't changed a bit since we last parted company. Well, as it so happens I have brought along a princess…no no, don't interrupt me, this time I have a real one and she is coming to take her rightful place. She slipped through the ball with ease and overcame the temptation of the money tree. I know she is a real one and I intend to take her to her deserved reward."

Suzy was uncertain what all this meant. She felt as though her presence was not as welcome as Emeralda had earlier indicated. She shifted her gaze to the lady whose eyes met hers. For a moment, she saw a deep darkness that made her shudder. Then Emeralda smiled at Suzy and said calmly, "Don't worry, my little precious princess. We are going down to the castle and you will be the ruler of all the land that you can see."

"Emeralda, I'll bet you haven't explained anything about this place to her. In fact, I know you haven't. This won't work. You can't bring an unsuspecting child and expose her to the tests that await her," the old man said, his voice rumbling.

"Marlen, stop it!" ordered Emeralda. "You will frighten the precious one with your nattering. I will go with her, guide her, protect her and see that she gets all that is rightfully hers."

"I can see it all now," said the old man, "You just want it all for yourself. You intend to manipulate this little one so you can get your hands on the lodestone. It won't work. Don't try it. Can't you remember what happened the last time you tried this? Obviously, you do not care about the safety of this little one, do you, Emeralda?"

"Nonsense, old fool. We are going now," shouted Emeralda. She took Suzy's hand and led her down the path to a ledge. As she stood there, she whispered to Suzy, "Just leave it up to me. Let yourself go and we will float down and over the board to the castle."

Suzy felt the Sage release her from her grasp and then she felt something strange happening. Her stomach seemed to float and fill with butterflies. She looked about and saw the landscape become twisted and stretched. She saw Emeralda become thin and contorted, like a piece of paper. She heard her whisper, "Come child, just relax and let it take you. We'll be together."

Suzy felt a sense of calm come over her as her body seemed to roll up like a blind. She looked about and saw Marlen high up on the hill looking down at them. His arm was out-stretched and he was shaking his head. Suddenly, Suzy felt uneasy. She wondered what was wrong with this place. Nothing seemed right. Her mind went back to the schoolroom and she again saw the geometric tools—the set squares, compass and protractor. She knew that this place did not fit with what she had studied. She could hear Emeralda screaming at her for thinking about those real objects. The Sage exhorted Suzy to put her mind in Emeralda's hands. All of a sudden, Suzy saw the landscape snap back into perspective and saw a black shadow speed off towards the castle, followed by a piercing scream. Suzy shuddered at the sound of that shriek and instinctively knew she had to flee.

Suzy quickly ran back up the slope to Marlen. He spoke quickly, "Well done, little princess. You indeed are one but it is not safe for you here now. Emeralda will be returning soon and she will try to stop you from leaving. Go back the way you came and stay true to the course set out for you. We may meet again."

Suzy nodded her head in thanks and retraced her footsteps along the path. Ahead of her were the money trees but they no longer looked as they had before. Instead, the grove looked dark and sinister, and the branches drooped closely to the ground. She could hear a moaning sound coming from the trees. She approached cautiously and could make out horrid laughter and threats being directed towards her. She tried to see a way through but each time that she approached the branches would drop lower and conceal the path. She could see no other way through the trees. Her thoughts returned to the little church that served as her worship home and she saw the Bible and the picture of the Saviour. Under the picture were the words 'I am the way, the truth and the life." As she remembered this passage, she felt confident and moved forward. Instead of dipping, the branches flinched and withdrew from her, clearing a path and allowing her to leave that place, but not without groaning and screaming at her. Suzy hoped she could find her way through the rest of this maze. Ahead of her loomed another challenge.

The oak tree seemed immense and about to pounce on her. She tried to edge by but the fragrance of the mistletoe began to overwhelm her. She felt heady and a bit giddy. She seemed to be looking through a fog and she could see the mistletoe reaching out for her. It seemed to be all right because it was saying lovely things. She spotted Emeralda coming swiftly down the path. Her mind turned to home and she saw the kitchen with her loving parents. She felt the ground spin out from under her and she drifted off into a sleep of contentment.

Suzy opened her eyes and saw the circus being assembled at the foot of the hill. Her back rested against the flat stone of her throne as she had called it. She smiled and stood up. 'What a delightful and strange dream,' she thought. 'I guess I had better go home for lunch.'

With that Suzy, her parent's little princess, skipped off on her way home leaving behind the circus and its strange and delightful adventures.

-2-

On her way home Suzy cut across the meadow, crawled under the fence and hopped over the narrow ditch along side the road. She paused for a moment to observe a killdeer, which scurring away from her, feigning a broken wing. Suzy almost fell for the age-old trick by following the poor helpless bird, but remembered what her dad had told her about that marvelous bird. She decided to look about to find the nest and carefully searched the roadside. After a few minutes she spotted the speckled eggs in the feather-lined nest and pondered the fate of the soon to be hatched birds. Then she walked away, aware of the ever-present scolding the mother was delivering. She knew this was the mother's display of her protective instinct for her offspring.

The road made its way down a slope into a hollow, filled with fruit trees and nourished by the presence of water from the tiny brook that wound along the bottom of the ravine. Suzy paused for a few minutes on the small bridge that crossed the stream and watched the minnows that darted back and forth in the water. She emitted a little scream when the water splashed as a rainbow trout flipped through the air. She chuckled to herself to relieve the embarrassment she felt at having been frightened by the fish. She watched but could no longer observe the trout. She leaned against the railing and gazed about at the tranquil scene before her. Many of the wild fruit trees were laden with berries, of varying in colours indicating the degree of ripeness. Plumb blue saskatoons weighed down many branches while other limbs held clusters of red, green and white berries. Intermingled with these were bunches of rose hips and unripened hazel nuts. 'Everything has a time to ripen,' she thought.

Suzy moved on. Part way up the hill she looked off to the left to see the large pond formed by a small dam that had been placed across one of the tributary ravines. The village used this for its drinking water. It also served as a swimming hole for most of the children in the neighbourhood.

Out of the corner of her eye she saw a black shadow swooping down on her. A closer glance showed it to be Emeralda and Suzy responded by running as fast as she could. As Suzy ran, she glanced again over her shoulder and saw the lady in black gaining on her. She saw malice in her eyes: the emerald earring seemed to deepen and beckon. Suddenly the lady was off her feet gliding through the air, with her arms outstretched and bearing down on the fleeing girl.

When Suzy thought she would pounce, the lady veered to the left and upward. Suzy brought herself to a sudden stop. She looked up in amazement into the regal but friendly face of an elderly gentleman wearing a tall pointed hat, adorned with stars and different symbols. He had his arm upraised and grasped in his fist a long gray wooden staff that he shook three times at the black figure. Suzy looked again in the direction of the lady and saw only a large crow streaking away. She saw something bright and green fall from the sky as the crow shrieked and tried to circle back to reclaim its loss. The presence of the old man scared it off and the bird disappeared over the rise in the land.

Suzy looked at the old man who smiled at her. "Oh, Marlen, if you had not been here I am afraid that I could not have run hard enough!"

Marlen laughed and patted his stomach, "No, my little one, you were quite safe, even without me here. Emeralda has no control over you now but she wanted to make your life unpleasant by scaring you. She had her chance earlier but you remained firm in what you believed, even if you did not realize it. That's one of the wonders of childhood—you haven't learned to be cynical and doubting." Marlen put his hand on Suzy's shoulder and Suzy responded with a giggle.

"What did Emeralda want with me?" Suzy asked.

Marlen paused and looked off into the distance and his face became saddened by whatever he saw. After a very long moment he turned to Suzy and said, "You are so very young but Emeralda knew that you were one of the special ones—princesses we call them. Somehow each princess is born with the ability to move freely between worlds and have at their touch some unique power to manipulate their surroundings."

Suzy interjected, "But I don't have any special powers...."

Marlen held up his hand and continued, "None that you know of at this time, my child. However, before I carry on I must give you a little advice. You are a princess and as such, you must learn to conduct yourself as one. You cannot be interrupting your elders, even if we are to be your servants. You must also learn to distinguish between friend and foe by acting with more thought and care."

Suzy hung her head in silent embarrassment. She wanted to argue but something about Marlen indicated to her that such activity would be most inappropriate. At the same time, his words were having a profound effect.

Marlen waited a moment before continuing, noting that his

little advice had had some effect on this young and inexperienced special child. "Yes, child, you do have a very special gift which even I can not recognize at this time. In due course, it will become evident and then you will fulfill your destiny, either here or in Gorn, or both. Oh yes, special one, that's the name of that place that you just visited before it was your time."

Suzy waited for a pause before she started to speak, "Just where is this Gorn? How did I get there? Will I ever go back?"

Marlen chuckled and with a smile he replied, "One question at a time, little one. You cannot find Gorn on a map here. It is right here along with this world and how many others, I cannot say. Windows between the two worlds open occasionally and one can briefly see from one into the other. Some of these windows are only one way so that people can see the other world. Other times two way viewing is possible; then people in the two worlds have attempted to communicate with each other, with varying levels of success. Gateways between the two worlds do exist—usually in multiples. Passing through different gateways usually takes you to other locations, such as happened to you. You entered through a captured gateway—the one in Emeralda's viewing ball, and came out in the glade. When you returned, you dropped through the gate at the mistletoe and came out by the rock."

"Marlen, I thought it was all a dream. I'm sure I fell asleep and dreamt the whole thing."

Marlen sighed and chuckled. "People of your world are so rational—reluctant to believe that some things happen because of forces that can not be explained by reasoning. You think you dreamt all of this. That is the way Emeralda meant it to be. She knew that you would be a difficult ward to handle and she planned that if you were to slip through her fingers she would have a contingency plan, a back up plan. Emeralda is like a spider; she weaves a web that has many ways to travel and many sticky spots that act as traps. She has to be watched with care anytime that she is nearby. She also does not give up easily." Marlen held up his hand, as Suzy was ready to ask another question.

-3-

Suzy looked at Marlen with admiration and astonishment. She knew she should be quiet but she went ahead with her question. "Why did she do that? She seemed like such a nice lady but she kept demanding that I follow her instructions."

Marlen placed his hand on her shoulder. "Emeralda can seem to be a very pleasant person but don't let looks deceive you. She is cunning and vicious; she will try to trap anyone, friend or foe. She wanted you so she could get what she wanted, what she has always wanted, and what she has been working for such a very long time without much success up until now."

"Is she really evil?" Suzy asked.

Marlen paused. He returned his gaze to his young friend, "Yes, evil has taken control of her. She is also very determined. Once she has set out on a course of action she will pursue it without giving up—unless she already knows that she has been beaten. You look terrified, little princess, and well you should when faced with a foe like her...."

"But Marlen," Suzy gasped," I don't want to be her foe. I want to be friends with everyone and...." She stopped and blushed. "I'm sorry, there I go again, interrupting you and not minding my manners. I really don't know how I shall ever overcome such a habit and...." Again she turned a deeper shade of red as she realized what she was doing.

Marlen just waited for her to stop and then gave her shoulder a little squeeze. "Oh, little princess, you have a lot to learn and it must be tough when all of this is thrust your way. Nevertheless, while you may wish to be friends with everyone you cannot be. That is just the way it is in the dark worlds. I have been in many, and they are all the same in that regard. We must simply do the best that we can. Emeralda now knows that she can never have power over you because you defeated her attempt to lure you into a trap. She believed that if she called you to her place while you were very young she might pull it off. Now, however, she will continue to bother you and try to frighten you away whenever she senses a danger from you."

Suzy just stood there, hearing these words and somehow realizing them to be true, but not really understanding any of it. Finally she could hold back no longer and she blurted out, "But, Marlen, what do I have that she wants? Why would an old woman want what belongs to a young girl?"

Marlen smiled with feeling and compassion, "It's not what you have, but who you are."

"But I'm just a simple country girl who lives with her parents who farm some land and raise some chickens and milk some cows. I've always wanted a baby brother or sister but that hasn't happened. I go to school in a small two-room schoolhouse that was there when my parents went to school. On Sundays, we go to the only church in town—a small white building with a bell tower that reaches right up to the sky. A lot of us kids joke that God can never forget when we have services because the bells ring right outside of heaven. Oh, please Marlen, tell me why Emeralda wants me. I haven't done anything to harm her."

Marlen just nodded as Suzy ended her plea. He cleared his throat and with a sweep of his hand continued his explanation of the wrong doings of the lady in black.

"Emeralda doesn't want any of your possessions, little one. She has more than she knows what to do with. No, if she wanted more material belongings she has the means at her disposal to accomplish that end."

Marlen thought about the best way to explain why Emeralda had come to see her. He knew that she was very young and might find the reasons too confusing. The consequences of her learning the truth might be more than she could handle. Yet, he knew this girl had proven her inner strength in the short battle with Emeralda and that she had done it on her own, much to Emeralda's chagrin. He could sense she wanted to know more and that the truth was a necessity.

He began, "Emeralda is not a child of this world where you make your home. She comes from a world, not unlike yours in many ways, called Gorn. I have already mentioned that before. However, Gorn is as of yet an unsaved place and the forces of evil wrestle every day for complete mastery. I am a Sage and a member of a group that opposes the evil forces. We would keep Gorn at peace so the bounty of Gorn could be shared with all the people. We have developed many tools and devices to aid us, the greatest of which is the lodestone. Often the enemy tries to construct a counter-device so we must never relax. These instruments can be very scary—we must keep them under control.

Suzy sat down on a large rock by the roadside, mesmerized by the story. Marlen waited for Suzy to become comfortable. He was concerned after all she had been through and he still had much to tell her.

"Emeralda is part of the dark force, although she originally was a Sage. She once worked to maintain harmony, but greed turned her from her original purpose. She guarded the lodestone and maintained the field around it. She was vigilant through the first watch, a period of one hundred and eleven years. She was asked to repeat the cycle since her replacement was unavailable. She remained true to her task and was to be relieved by another Sage at the end of the second watch. However, the dark forces had mounted an offensive to break out of their region. All the Sages were occupied at the end of the second cycle in this renewed battle. We decided to permit Emeralda to complete a third cycle. No Sage had ever been asked to do this before, yet Emeralda seemed the logical choice since she had done so well. In retrospect, it was an unwise move on our part. We gave no thought to the strain that more than two guardianships would have. We were caught in the midst of a battle and felt we had no other choice.

As time passed we sensed fluctuations in the field that surrounded the lodestone, but when we investigated it was always at full strength. Emeralda maintained the field had remained unbroken and we had no reason to distrust her. She seemed to become more reclusive and withdrawn as the third cycle progressed. The council of Sages saw this happening but a guardian had never been removed mid-cycle. Emeralda remained on her appointed task. What an error on our part! We might have prevented the transformation, but we feared the effect on a Sage who had been denied the opportunity to complete a given task."

Suzy's eyes had grown wide with astonishment at the story that Marlen was relating. He had held the youngster spellbound. It all seemed like a fairy tale, yet something about Marlen let her know that she was hearing the facts without exaggeration. Suzy wanted to interrupt the story to ask little questions but it was as though Marlen anticipated each. She decided to sit back and take it all in.

"Suddenly the council knew that the lodestone had been violated. The field ceased to exist—the Sages had collectively worked to keep it in place and their effort was no longer needed. I was sent at once. The closer I came to the lodestone the weaker I became. Still I strove onward and finally dragged myself into the lodestone room—the room that had been so carefully constructed to prevent thievery or sabotage. The stone was still there but on the floor beside the pedestal that had been created for it. Emeralda lay beside the stone, comatose with eyes of death. Her hands revealed what had transpired. They were burned deeply with the bluish tinge of the lodestone. The air reeked of burnt flesh. I summoned all my strength to mindlink with the rest of the Sages who sent a group to the rescue of the lodestone. Upon seeing the effect of the lodestone on a Sage, a box was built over it until a means could be developed to move it properly. The room was sealed off using the field. Emeralda was transported to the Sage Palace where the finest doctors and all the Sages worked to rescue her from the malady that gripped her. She remained rigid, almost in a death-like paralysis, until near the end of the cycle. During that time, she tossed and turned so violently that she had to be restrained using golden chains and clamps. She would scream and utter guttural curses so vile that those present were sickened upon hearing them. She began to chant in the most ancient language of Gorn, a series of grunts and moans, even though her training had never included language studies. We feared for her life and had we known what was to come later we might not have strived so hard to save her. But, still to be fair, we had to bear the responsibility for having left her with the stone for so very long.

As the cycle ended she became very tranquil and showed a marked improvement. We were relieved only to find that on the day of the new cycle we had a new Emeralda who had become greedy, demanding and very selfish. She talked of nothing but having the chance to control and hold the lodestone. We warned her of the dangers. She exploded angrily that it was unfair to deny what rightfully belonged to her.

The Council decided that she had to be confined for her sake and for the safety of all. As plans were being made, Emeralda escaped from our protection and began her quest to overcome and control the stone."

"Wouldn't that have been dangerous to her?" Suzy asked.

"Oh yes, but she was possessed with the need and desire to fulfill that ambition. It consumed her and she could think of nothing else. She is still like that. She somehow learned that there are some very special people, princes and princesses they came to be called, that can hold and manipulate the stone. Where she gained this information, we do not know, unless it came from the stone itself or from some aspect of the dark. These special people do not live in Gorn but in worlds adjacent to Gorn. Movement between the worlds had long been known but had been limited to the Sages. Now Emeralda used her lore to cross over to find these special people. Why some people should have the ability to control the lodestone is unknown but then the Sages do not claim to know everything. We only know what we have learned from the old masters, from the books they left and from our first hand experiences. Emeralda succeeded in gaining control over the stone through a princess known as Ebony. Ebony was found by Emeralda and came under her control. Ebony was able to enter the lodestone room, open the special box and remove the lodestone from its resting place. Emeralda secreted it away to the Grey Hills where she built a huge castle. For many years with

Ebony at her side, she increased her power. She carved out a sizable dominion for herself, which she used to thwart the Sages and the dark side. She came to believe that she could control the dark forces using the power of the stone. Her shortsightedness lay in her lack of knowledge of Ebony's nature. As the years passed, Ebony changed, matured and then began to age. Emeralda did not make much of it at first. She just assumed that Ebony would always be there the way she had been. Ebony remained firmly committed to controlling the stone for Emeralda because she knew that this was the source of her prestige and power. However, as she aged she grew cantankerous and more selfish than ever. She would argue with Emeralda—if Emeralda threatened her, she would sulk and withdraw to one of her rooms and refuse to see her mistress until Emeralda would come bearing a gift. Both were frustrated by each other yet each needed the other to survive. Ebony made sure that she got all that she could from their relationship. When Ebony began to move slower, think harder and forget more often, Emeralda became concerned. She began to study other members of Ebony's world, which by the way, is this place.

The Sages knew something was amiss within the camp of Emeralda when she would disappear for long periods of time. Ebony maintained a degree of control over Emeralda because she was needed but she was fast becoming unstable and was drifting to the edge of senility. The Sages knew that great change was about to occur but were very concerned about the direction that it would take. If Emeralda were successful in her mysterious, secretive quest then her power would grow and she would prove to be uncontrollable and unbeatable. If Ebony became uncontrollable or unstable, then the danger of misguided use of the lodestone could result. Moreover, there was the possibility that the dark forces would choose the right moment to strike and this would result in the loss of the lodestone and an even greater catastrophe for Gorn.

I was dispatched by the council to follow Emeralda. My quest brought me to this world after a long absence"

Marlen stopped talking and gazed out across the hills for a moment as though he were lost in a distant memory.

-4-

Marlen turned to Suzy after a moment of reflection. He placed his hand on her shoulder and smiled. "This world was quite different when I first came here. It was greener, cleaner and much more simple. People were content with a lot less and seemed to enjoy themselves more. It was in this tranquil place that I had the task of searching for Emeralda and discerning her task. I suspected, as did most of the Council, that it had something to do with the changes that had happened to Ebony but I had no idea where my search would lead. Emeralda's trail was not hard to pick up. She seemed to cause a disturbance anywhere she made her presence known. I moved cautiously and soon discovered that this world was not accustomed to our ways. We have the means to move quickly from one location to another. We can be present in a location without disturbing the outward appearance of that spot. We can manipulate the surroundings without being observed. People of this world apparently have not had such things happen in their more recent past and are quite upset when it occurs. They refer to it as magic or sorcery. Emeralda either did not know that her activities were disturbing or she chose to ignore the uproar she caused. I was very careful to appear as one of the people of this place and to avoid doing anything that would be disturbing. I soon gained the confidence of many individuals and learned a great deal about this place. In some ways, it has many attributes that make it superior to Gorn. However, I had to determine why Emeralda had come here. On many occasions, I noticed her, without her knowledge, observing young girls. She would spend a great deal of time studying their movements and then she would set up little tests for them. Most were frightened off by the tasks that were presented to them. A few would try and then run away when the tasks became more difficult. One young girl moved through the battery of activities with ease and became more aggressive and agile as she proceeded. I was concerned that, perhaps, Emeralda had discovered what she sought. Emeralda then took the next step and appeared before the young girl, who screamed and at first was quite frightened. However, her curiosity and Emeralda's adept maneuvering convinced the child to go along with the next test.

Marlen stood up and said, "I have been talking long enough. I want you to actually see what happened next. Suzy, stand up and look over here. I want you to look at this clump of wildflowers and watch how they move as I tell you the story."

Suzy was puzzled but she did as she was told and relaxed as Marlen continued the story.

"Emeralda then took the girl to Gorn…"

Suzy saw Emeralda leading a blond haired girl by the hand through some very rugged terrain. The Sage stopped and looked around before she started down a path towards a pool of water fed by a waterfall. Emeralda very carefully stepped over the wet stones and guided the young girl along the path. She stopped and again looked around. She then led her ward along a ledge that took them behind the cascading water.

Suzy was fascinated with the drama that was unfolding before her eyes. She watched as the two travelers walked through the tunnel into a hidden valley. A large castle stood in the centre of the valley. Emeralda turned to the girl and said, "This is my castle in the heart of the Grey Hills. Here I have the lodestone, my precious baby. I need your help to take it away from an old woman who won't let me come close."

The girl turned towards Emeralda and Suzy gasped. "Marlen, this girl does not have a face. I can't continue to watch her because I will wonder about her features rather than paying attention to your story."

Marlen sighed. "I had hoped that you would not notice. I should have known better. For reasons I wish to keep to myself I have left her faceless. However, for your sake I will give her your face and we will call her Suzytwo."

Suzy laughed as she saw herself with Emeralda. Then she shuddered as she remembered the last time she had been pursued by that Sage. 'Oh well, this is just a story.' She watched as Suzytwo and the lady in black walked towards the Castle. She also noticed that Marlen had followed the pair but had remained hidden from view within the tunnel.

Emeralda led the young girl into the castle and went directly to the room with the lodestone. Ebony came out of an adjoining room and screamed at Emeralda when she saw Suzytwo. "How dare you come here with this brat? Did you think you could just walk in here and I would not know? I have no idea what you had in mind, Emeralda, but I cannot let you come any closer to this precious baby." Ebony waved her walking stick at Suzytwo who retreated behind the Sage. Ebony cackled at the young girl's response.

"Step out of the way, Ebony. Suzytwo is here to perform some of the tasks that you refuse to do. I do not have time to stand here in a discussion with you."

"You treacherous witch. You brought me here and you used me, over and over. I am your servant and I have no intention of stepping aside for another, especially this cowardly little imp." Ebony stepped forward and raised her stick. She began to swing it back and forth. Suzytwo stepped back again as danger approached.

Emeralda scowled and raised her hand. She tapped her staff twice on the floor, while muttering some words in a language that Suzy did not understand. Ebony stopped swinging her stick and words ceased to pour out of her mouth. Suzy watched as Emeralda led Suzytwo around the now paralyzed Ebony to the stone.

"See the beautiful stone—it is the reason I brought you here. You can become a powerful ruler of all this land if you will take the stone away from here. We will set up a new castle to house the lodestone and we will take control of all of Gorn. You will be its queen."

Suzytwo looked around and then gazed at the lodestone. She appeared to hesitate, as if in deep thought. Suzy wanted to shout at her not to listen to Emeralda, but she realized that she could not be heard. She was viewing an event that had happened in the past. Suzytwo smiled and Emeralda nodded, pointing towards the lodestone.

"You will be the richest person in all of Gorn. You will have servants and the finest clothing. It's all yours if you simply take the stone," Emeralda cooed.

Suzytwo stepped forward and reached out towards the stone. The stone throbbed, emitting green, yellow and blue hues. Suzytwo placed her hands around the lodestone to pick it up. As she did her face contorted with pain and she screamed in agony. Her hands were blackened and the air was filled with the stench of burning flesh. Emeralda grabbed a vase containing flowers, threw them on the floor and poured the water over Suzytwo's hands. Suzytwo moaned in anguish and Ebony shrieked with dirision at her mistress. "You deceitful witch! You thought you could replace me with this weakling! When will you learn that you need me? I promise you will pay dearly for this treachery." Ebony danced around Emeralda and the moaning girl. "Get her out of my sight," Ebony ordered.

Suzy watched as Emeralda picked up Suzytwo, threw her over her shoulder like a sack of potatoes and walked out of the castle. She did not return through the tunnel but passed through a portal near the moat. Suzy watched as Marlen came out of the tunnel and walked across the yard to where Emeralda had left. He looked towards the castle, listened to Ebony's cackling and then he stepped through the gateway.

Suzy saw him emerge and hurry towards a bundle lying on the edge of the road. Suzy saw at once that it was Suzytwo. Emeralda had brought her back but had abandoned her in her pain and misery. Emeralda was nowhere to be seen. Marlen picked up Suzytwo and carried her across the road and into a small shed that stood some distance away. Suzy watched as Marlen placed Suzytwo on a table and began to examine the horrible burns. He picked up a bucket that was lying there and went out to the stream that flowed through the field to get some water. As he returned he stopped several times, picking various plants and flowers. When he returned to the shed he took a white cloth from a pocket and placed it in the water. He carefully cleaned the charred hands.

Suddenly the door opened and a boy entered the shed. He shouted, "What have you done to her?" He began to beat the Sage with his fists yelling, "Stay away from her. Don't you dare harm her anymore."

Marlen seized the young man by his wrists and quietly asked, "Could you stop shouting? It is very hard on your friend here. Let me assure you I did not hurt her. I found her with her hands badly burned and I am trying to ease her pain. You can help by stopping your attack and assisting me in healing these terrible wounds. Will you do that for her?"

Suzy noticed the boy too was faceless and she did not interrupt Marlen's story to ask why. She simply projected the features of her best friend on him and he became Timmytwo. Timmytwo nodded to Marlen who smiled and released his wrists. Marlen waved towards the table and asked, "Would take those plants and flowers, remove the leaves and petals and place them in the water in the bucket? Stir the mixture with the stems of the reddish flowers. I will need them in a few minutes. He turned back to continue cleaning the charred hands. Timmytwo began the task that had been requested without hesitation.

When Marlen completed the cleaning chore he turned to see Timmytwo stirring the mixture as he had requested. Marlen removed a small bottle from one of his pockets and carefully placed three drops of an orange liquid into the bucket. The contents began to bubble as Timmytwo continued to stir it. When he lifted his hands he gasped to see the flower stems had dissolved into the mixture. Marlen said, "Its ready. Don't be afraid—the potion will not harm your friend." Marlen placed the cloth into the mixture so it became soaked with the fluid. He then placed this on the charred hands and gently pressed it against the burnt flesh. A light moan came from Suzytwo's lips.

Marlen indicated that Timmytwo should continue the process while Marlen placed his hands on Suzytwo's head and he closed his eyes. Suzytwo stopped moaning. Timmytwo was amazed to seen the charring disappear and a healthy colour return to his friend's hands. He did not stop placing the dampened cloth on her hands until Marlen opened his eyes and said, "That's all for now. I believe we have completed the healing." He removed his hands from the girl's head and smiled. "Well done, young man, your assistance was greatly needed."

Timmytwo asked, "How did you do that?"

"I am a Sage. I have trained as a healer. This is one of my jobs. Look! Your friend is coming to."

Suzytwo opened her eyes and stared at her two companions. She looked at her hands and then at Marlen.

Timmytwo spoke first, "Marlen found you with some very burned hands. He has just healed them."

"Timmytwo helped me do that. He must be a very good friend."

Suzy heard Marlen ask her to pay attention to him. She lifted her eyes from the wildflowers and looked at the old man, who continued the story.

"The girl had not been told that there was any danger. As I talked to these young people, I soon discovered that they had hidden traits that I had not noticed before. Emeralda had discovered the girl and had used some tests. I decided to carry out some of my own investigations. I was amazed to find that both of these children possessed untapped strengths and abilities. I realized that Emeralda had been in a hurry and had acted hastily and prematurely. I realized that these two could be powerful allies against the lady in black if they were properly trained.

It took quite some time to work with these young people but it was much easier than I first thought. They grasped the hidden meanings and soon began to make use of their hidden talents. I discovered that they did not require the usual mandatory training since they knew what was right and what was wrong. It was thrilling to see them grow in their abilities within the limits imposed by the Council of Sages. They already knew the limits and often their sense was much more rigid and demanding than the Sages had ever contemplated. I often thought that the Council would have done well if they had had the opportunity to be exposed to those two. Enough of that. Without going into long details, the time soon came when I knew they were ready for the task that lay ahead.

You can once again turn your attention to the flower patch and see what happened next," Marlen said.

Suzy saw Suzytwo and Timmytwo enter Gorn through a gateway that brought them out near the Castle in the Grey Hills. Marlen urged them to enter the castle. Timmytwo followed Suzytwo who knew the way to the room with the lodestone. Ebony appeared before them and shrieked, "Why are you here? Little yellow hair, you did not learn from your last visit. I will not let you in." Ebony raised a long pointed stick and began to move towards them. Suzytwo and Timmytwo looked at each other, nodded and began to run. Ebony was after them at once and for a short time was able to keep up the pace. However, she soon tired and began to pant for air. She sat down on a stool to catch her breath.

The two young people left her to rest and entered the room with the lodestone. They both stared at the magnificent stone before Timmytwo stepped forward and picked up the stone. Suzytwo gasped as his hands made contact with the lodestone. She was amazed that he was able to handle it without harm. They walked out of the room and saw that Ebony still was seated and unable to physically stop them.

Ebony screamed at them. "Thieves! What are you doing? You can't take our precious treasure." She cursed them for coming into her castle but she was unable to prevent their movements.

"Ebony, why are you screaming?" a voice came from down the hall.

"Its Emeralda," Suzytwo whispered to her friend. "She will try to stop us for sure. Let's stay close together. Remember, she is a liar and she will do all that she can to stop us."

"I'm coming, Ebony," Emeralda said from a hall nearby as Ebony kept up her tirade. Emeralda entered the room and came to a sudden stop as she saw the young people with the lodestone. She stood stark still and a frown formed on her face. Her eyes moved from the boy with the stone to the young girl. She changed the frown into a pleasant smile as she addressed the intruders.

"I don't know how you made it back here, sweet princess, but I can see I was very mistaken about your abilities. You have brought a friend with you and he has the power to handle the lodestone. I am so pleased to see the two of you. You have a great future in store for both of you now that you have the lodestone under your control. With my help, we can take complete control of Gorn—Chrane and the Sages will be unable to stand against the kingdom the three of us will form. With my help you will have riches and clothes and possessions beyond your wildest imaginations."

"Witch! You deceitful hag!" shrieked Ebony. "You promised all these to me and you have failed to deliver them. Now you are giving away my kingdom to these two imps. You can't do this. I will stop you."

Suzy was astonished at Ebony's vehemence. She almost laughed when she heard the promises Emeralda made to Timmytwo and Suzytwo. She had heard them herself when Emeralda lured her into Gorn. She settled back as Marlen continued his story.

"Be quiet, Ebony. You haven't had it bad all this time. You will be included," Emeralda said in a condescending voice.

"I'm to trust you. I don't and I won't." Ebony advanced towards the two young people waving her stick dangerously. She came to a sudden stop as she looked past Emeralda and saw

Marlen had entered the room. Emeralda followed her gaze and blanched at the sight of the Sage.

"Please don't take my baby from me. I can't live without her. I will do whatever I must if you will leave the lodestone here," she beseeched Marlen as she crumbled to her knees.

"Emeralda, you must promise right now that you will not harm these young people and that you will not attempt to escape. A group of Sages are on their way here right now to place you in custody," Marlen ordered.

Emeralda collapsed to the floor and whimpered her agreement with the order she had received. She moaned pathetically as Ebony began to scream and laugh at her.

"Look at the mighty Emeralda. You were going to rule the world. You promised me wealth and position but you cannot free yourself. What a fraud!"

Marlen beckoned to the young people to follow him and Suzy watched as they left the prisoners behind. As they emerged from the castle Suzy saw a group of people clothed in bright robes coming up the steps. Marlen spoke to them.

"You came at once."

"We received your message and knew it was urgent. Where is Emeralda?" one of the Sages asked.

"She is inside the castle with Ebony. She has promised to remain and that will hold her for now. I propose that we cast a spell over the castle to confine Emeralda and Ebony. In that way we will be rid of Emeralda as a problem. We will provide all the necessities for life. In the meantime I will lead these young people to the lodestone castle and restore the force field around the stone."

Suzy watched as Timmytwo and Suzytwo followed Marlen away from the Grey Hills. The Sages set about casting spells over the castle. She looked up from the patch of flowers because Marlen had stopped relating his story.

"The stone was returned to the special vault and the spells were restored," Marlen continued. "The prince and the princess toured Gorn for a short time and then were transported back at their request. Emeralda remained under castle confinement with her charge—a more fitting penalty could not have been devised. Ebony made her life miserable right up to the end and we became aware of another way in which people of your world differ from those of Gorn. You are released from this form after a lifetime.

Emeralda remained a prisoner until the Dark Force grew in strength and the Sages' attention was diverted elsewhere. We had cast the spell over Emeralda and Ebony confining them to the castle. With Ebony gone the spell ceased and Emeralda was free to resume her wicked quest. One of her tries involved you and thus here we are."

Suzy shook her head as she tried to take in everything that Marlen had just related to her. She struggled for the right words. "I know that she can be so deceiving and cunning but there is something about her that makes me feel so very sorry for her. Deep inside her must be a terrible hurt that has poisoned an otherwise wonderful person. I do wish there was someway to help her, to restore her to that wonderful person that she was before. If only there was something I could do."

Marlen smiled again and said, "I knew there was something special about you. You have such a caring heart. You do not want to see the evil that Emeralda displays on the outside by her terrible deeds—you look deep within to see the remnants of a once magnificent Sage. The Sages have tried all they could to heal her but came up short because Emeralda blocked their actions and their probing. Unless she permits a change to occur I am afraid, there is nothing that can be done. Maybe someone else can reach her but I would be wary that she might bring harm to that person. You, however, are a gem, my dear."

Marlen stopped talking, smiled and put his arm around Suzy who snuggled in close to this dear man who only a short time ago had seemed to be frightening and strange. She looked out across the field and she thought she saw a sparkle. Suzy ran out into the field where she had seen the glittering reflection. She reached down and picked up an earring stud—one with a bright shinning emerald at one end. It was beautiful and glowed as Suzy looked at it. She seemed mesmerized by it as she made her way back to Marlen on the side of the road. He frowned as he saw what the girl had recovered.

"You know to whom that belongs, don't you?" he asked quietly.

"Yes, I do," murmured the girl, "I saw Emeralda wearing it when we went into Gorn. You know she said that if I ever needed her help she would be there for me."

"Of course, she said that then. She was in control, or so she thought. She was quick to offer to help you to do as she wished. Why she dropped this gem, I do not know, but I am sure it was no accident. Yet, maybe it can come to some good. We cannot just leave it in the field because it does not belong there. If you have it, you may find it useful in calling on Emeralda to be of assistance. She will have no choice but to help."

Suzy looked puzzled. "Why would she want to help me by leaving the jewel behind?"

Marlen put his hands together and brought them to his lips, pausing as if in deep thought. Then he said, "She likely has some thought of getting revenge on you or even getting you back under her control. I doubt that is possible, but her mind is no longer clear and that may not have come to her yet. In any case, be wary and only use the earring if it is absolutely necessary."

Marlen reached up to his neck and removed a tiny golden chain that hung there. "Here, let's fasten that gem to this chain so that you can wear it around your neck until you get home. Find a safe place to keep it, little princess, lest it fall in the hands of someone who may be harmed by it."

Suzy admired the chain and gem a moment and then shuddered involuntarily as she slipped it over her head. She felt a cold shiver run down her back. She began to remove it when Marlen held up his hand.

She stopped and looked at him. "I really don't think I want this thing. I will never use it to call that evil woman. I would be too frightened of her."

"Emeralda is indeed an evil woman but remember I told you she was once a Sage. She is still bound by many of the vows that Sages must take after years of preparation. Keep the earring, but put it aside. Its purpose is not for now but will be of use sometime later on. I gave you my chain so that if you ever need to call Emeralda I also will hear the call. I may not be able to come immediately but I will be aware that Emeralda has been summoned. You are a princess and have immense powers of which, at present, you are mostly unaware. Some of those powers manifested themselves in your first encounter with Gorn but they were used instinctively," Marlen explained slowly to his charge.

"My first encounter...will also be my last. I have no desire to go back," Suzy interjected.

"Perhaps you are right," Marlen said with a chuckle. "In the meantime I think you should hurry home because your dinner is waiting for you."

Suddenly Suzy looked surprised and a bit bewildered.

"I must be late already. I have been gone a long time."

"No, little one, you have been away only a moment. Gorn time and your time do not mesh. A long time here may be but a moment in Gorn and a long adventure in Gorn may occur as quickly as a thought in this place." Marlen gave Suzy a pat on her back. She turned and began to run towards home, which was just up the road and over the hill.

-5-

Suzy made her way up the short maple-lined lane from the road into the farmyard, that she called home. The little white cottage-style house was nestled in a flower garden, which in turn was surrounded by closely mown lawn. A tall majestic, symmetrical, blue spruce stood in the front yard, its trunk reaching skyward. Tucked in behind the house was a small red hip-roofed barn surrounded by white-framed corrals for the many farm animals that were raised in this place. Right now, however, Suzy was not interested in the idyllic setting that had been her home since birth. She was getting over the excitement of her adventure and she was filled with the desire to quickly relieve herself of her new found treasure. Her heart still beat with trepidation as she recalled the owner of the emerald ear stud. She grasped the golden chain and was immediately filled with relief as she remembered the white-haired, grandfatherly Marlen who had shown up at the exact moment she had needed help. Now, Suzy just wanted to get up to her room so that she could hide away this trinket in her favourite secret hiding spot.

She realized that it was very close to dinnertime. How would she get past her parents? Mom would spot the necklace. She never missed a thing. Again, Suzy touched the chain and all her fears evaporated. Somehow, she knew that it would all work out. After all, she had nothing to fear—she had not done anything wrong.

Suzy made her way up the steps and entered the little porch. She glanced to the right to see her mom busy putting bowls on the table. Her mom looked up and smiled.

"Suzy, go upstairs and wash up for dinner. Dad is in the washroom downstairs cleaning up and will be ready in a few minutes. Please don't dawdle. Everything is ready."

"I will be right down," Suzy replied and quickly made her way up the stairs that lead from the entryway. 'Mom hadn't noticed the necklace.' She went to the sink and washed herself adequately to pass the mother test. Then, very quietly, she entered her bedroom and went straight to the old oak chest of drawers that stood in a corner of the room. She opened the top drawer, reached in, and felt along the top until she found a thin boxlike structure. Gently she slid it to the side and removed it from its resting place. She set the shallowest drawer one could imagine on her bed and began to remove the chain from her neck. She had to hurry and a couple of times she brushed against the emerald. Each time she felt her stomach turn queasy. She dropped the necklace in the drawer, which she replaced in its hiding place.

She felt the urge to reach into the drawer and place the jewel in her hand. The temptation grew and she fought it, all the while becoming more desperate that her mom would call and start looking for her. She touched the chain and at once was able to put the drawer back in its proper location. She caught her breath as she slid the main drawer shut.

"Whew!" She exhaled loudly and turned to leave the room. Something kept calling out to her and she knew that she had to avoid the earring, especially right now.

In the dining room her mom looked up. "Didn't I tell you to go and wash up, sweetie?"

"Yes, Mom, you did and I have."

"Really! Come over here and let me check this out."

Suzy waited as she was inspected. "I'm truly amazed, little one. You, indeed, are clean and in such a short time. Your dad is still washing up. Please help me set out the dinner."

As the family was finishing up the apple crisp, Mom said, "The circus has come to town."

"Oh yes," Suzy said with a grin, "I watched it being set up from the hill that overlooks the village."

"I remember doing exactly the same thing when I was your age," her dad said. "I used to sit on the big rocks and watch as the tents were being set up. Your mom used to do that too."

'I'm sure you did not do exactly what I did this morning, dad.' Suzy thought. She was wrenched out of her thoughts by her father's next comment.

"There you are thinking that neither your mom nor your dad could ever have done anything like you, just because we are so old and could not possibly have had any fun when we were young." He winked at Mom, so openly that Suzy could not help but notice. He grinned from ear to ear. "You know both of us were once twelve just like you are. We used to sit on the top of that hill and survey the entire world and dream about what it would be like to rule over it all. We thought of it as our throne hill. Right, Mom?"

Suzy heaved a sign of relief when she realized that her dad was joking. For a moment, she had feared that he had been able to read her mind and had discovered her secret.

"That was a long time ago, before so many other things happened." Mom paused and for a moment, Suzy thought she had seen pain in her eyes. Dad lowered his eyes for a moment.

Mom continued, "It would be a treat if we could go into town later and see the circus. Circuses are so much fun; they remind me of what it was like when we were young."

Dad smiled. "A great idea! I have to go into town with the cream and eggs about three. Why don't you come in a bit later and we will meet at the circus and have some fun."

'Wow!' thought Suzy, 'First I have an adventure and now we are all going to the circus. I can't believe that all this is happening.'

"That sounds like fun, don't you agree, Suzy?" Mom asked, not expecting any answer but the daughter's smile. "Suzy and I will do up the inside chores after dinner and later, after I have a short nap, I will take her out to the garden to do a bit of weeding." Suzy frowned. "Come, come, little one, don't be so downhearted. Always a little work before we play. Life isn't all pleasure. Just think, if you really help out, maybe there'll be an extra treat later on."

The afternoon sped by, even with the little jobs that mom found for her to do. Suzy enjoyed being with her mom very much, so it was not a burden to help with the dishes and then spend time together in the garden. Her mom always shared so many delightful stories and events with her. Suzy particularly liked to hear her sing. Her mom had a beautiful voice and an amazing repertoire of songs. Suzy often joined her mother when she was encouraged to sing along.

"You have a lovely voice," her mom said. "With practice it can become the most beautiful voice in this area."

Suzy would imagine what it would be like to be a famous singer. She would help bring some income into the family and she could travel to far off places and see the world. Then she would feel a bit sad because she would no longer be at home and in close contact with her parents.

After dressing in skirts, blouses and bonnets, the two of them left the house about four-thirty. They walked to the village down the same road that Suzy had traveled in the morning. It was a pleasant afternoon and Suzy's mom had suggested the walk so that they could relax and enjoy the wonders of nature unfolding around them.

After a leisurely stroll, they came to the brink of the tall hill overlooking the circus. It was now completely set up, bustling with activity, and resounding with the sounds of animals, the circus master and the noise of many games. They descended the hill along the same path that Suzy had earlier traveled and entered the circus compound by the main gate. Suzy strained to see the tent with the stars and moons but it was nowhere to be seen.

"Gosh," said Suzy, "I was sure that there was a tent over there that had stars and moons on the doorway."

"I remember a tent just like that when I was a little girl. It was the place of business of an old fortune teller, a lady dressed in black," murmured her mom.

"What was the lady in black like?" a surprised Suzy asked.

"Oh, that was a long time ago," her mom said quietly. She looked at Suzy with a questioning look and peered for a long time into her daughter's eyes. "I think she went away and didn't return."

Suzy felt that her mom was not telling her everything. But her mom had always been forthright with her before. She did not have a chance to ask anymore questions.

"There's Dad waving at us," Mom said. "Let's hurry over and see what kind of an afternoon he has in mind for us."

The three of them went on to enjoy the main performance and many of the rides with their spins and loops. They also played several of the games where the operator tries to persuade you to part with your hard-earned cash by promising you that the next time you can trade in your little prize for a much larger one. Suzy was coached by her parents to see the technique that was being employed and she soon discovered that she had quite a knack for piling up the winnings and then withdrawing at the critical time. She enjoyed being able to walk away from the enticements that were placed before her and her parents complimented her on her self-control. She enjoyed herself. She knew that this day would be relived and enjoyed many times in the future.

At nine-thirty, the family returned home in the horse-drawn wagon. Suzy was fast asleep on her mother's lap, her head filled with the memories of the best circus ever. Her dad carried her up the stairs where her mom tucked her into bed and then rejoined her husband in the doorway. He placed his arms around her. Suzy slightly opened one eye and saw her parents standing there. She smiled with contentment and drifted off to sleep.

-6-

The garden plants had grown quickly in the heat of the summer, nurtured by the many pleasant showers, and the loving hands and care of Suzy and her mom. The pea pods hung heavily on the vine and called out for someone to reap the harvest. Suzy and her mom had answered the call in the morning and now while sitting in the shade of the large evergreen were shelling the peas. The peas shot out of the pods, as skilled fingers split open the cocoon in which the kernels had grown and then with a swipe of the finger, like the rapid movement of a filleting knife, the peas were freed from their tethers. It could be a long and tedious affair if you allowed yourself to get wrapped up in the mindless monotony of what seemed an endless task. However, if you used the time to retrieve memories, or had the company of someone who could share memories that were alive and vivid in detail, wonder and freshness, the time to process peas passed quickly. Suzy marveled at the wisdom of her mother as she related small anecdotes or expounded on the fascinating stories from the Bible. She never tired of hearing about the heroes, who through faith, were able to overcome what must have seemed at the time to be insurmountable obstacles. Some of her favourites were Joseph,

Ruth, Paul and Esther. Joseph, who was especially loved by his father, was betrayed by his brothers and sold into slavery. He persevered in exile and in prison, was released, became an important official and eventually had the chance once again to see his father and his family through faith. Ruth left her home after suffering the loss of her husband and followed her mother-in-law into a foreign land because of love and duty. She then was able to find a new love and a place in the new land because she had faith. Paul, who had persecuted so many, became a pillar of the new church and the expounder of the doctrines of faith. Esther, a Jewish girl in a foreign land, became a queen in the Persian Empire and saved her people because she had the courage and faith to challenge wrongful accusations before the King. Suzy looked at her mother and smiled. She too was a person of deep faith and courage who faced each day with joy and a smile.

Her mom looked up from her task and smiled at Suzy. "My, you sure seem to be lost in some serious thoughts today, sweetheart."

"I was just wondering," Suzy replied.

"What about?"

"Well, you seem to know so much. I can't help but wonder why you stayed here instead of going off to some college and becoming famous or something."

"Oh, Suzy, someday you will realize that being famous is not the most important thing in the world," her mom said gently.

Suzy sighed, "I know, Mother, you told me this many times but you have never answered my questions. Why didn't you leave? Did you not seek adventure?"

Her mom looked across the yard to the fields. She saw her husband in the field and smiled. "You are right, Suzy. I never have given you a satisfactory answer, not one for a young person like you. I've never really had the desire to leave this place and go somewhere to be famous. I grew up knowing your dad from very young and the two of us shared our youth together, an adventure in itself. We have done so many happy and enjoyable things together that I can't imagine what there could be anywhere else."

"I guess that's something I can't understand," Suzy said emphatically, "I want to be my own person."

"But I am my own person, Suzy. Your dad and I would never force the other to do anything against their will. That is hard to realize when you are young, but I know that my parents, your grandparents, also did the same thing. When I was your age, I did not see it. It was only as I matured that I realized you can both lean on, and support someone else."

Suzy smiled at her mom because she was impressed with the deep feelings she had for her dad, family and this place. She hoped that one day she too could experience that type of joy. However, right now she had the immense pleasure of hearing her mom say that since the peas had been shelled she could go out to play—as soon as, that is, the pea pods were given to the pigs.

Suzy pushed the wheelbarrow filled with the empty pods to the pig corral and enjoyed throwing pailfuls of pods to the pigs. They snorted with pleasure at this new food. She laughed as they would be startled when some of the pods landed on their snouts. When she completed the chore she wandered down the lane to the road and then she struck out across the pasture on the other side of the road. She came to the reservoir of the dam, which served as the source of water for the village. Trees of many kinds—maple, aspen, willow and birch bordered the water. Most were tall and thick trucked, well fed and watered.

Suzy liked to come to this place, which was so tranquil and serene—a good place to think about all of the important things in life. She sat down by the water and watched a Monarch butterfly as it fluttered by. She saw a small trout jump above the surface of the pond, its surface glistening silver. She looked up and there at her side stood Marlen. She had not heard him approach, but she was not frightened or startled by his sudden appearance.

"Hi, Marlen. It's been a long time since we last talked. See the trees are in full leaf and the sun is very warm. Summer is moving right along. How have you been since the last time we visited? I remember how you came to my rescue from that spooky and dangerous Emeralda. Is she still running around causing trouble? I feel sorry for her even though I know she is a mean witch of a person. I don't suppose...."

Marlen held up a hand to interrupt this very excited friend. He smiled as he thought about the talk on patience and decorum he had delivered the last time they were together, but he quickly decided not to bring up that topic now; at least, not for a little while. He looked around and found a willow trunk that ran in a horizontal direction on which to sit. He made himself comfortable, looked up and saw that Suzy was fidgeting and squirming with excitement.

"It has indeed been a long time. Not so long in your world but a great deal has occurred in Gorn. You know that time proceeds differently in Gorn. The dark side grew in strength and spread out from its eastern marches. We stalled its progress but were unable to drive it back to where it came from. Emeralda disappeared for a while and when she returned she was at the head of a force with a dark lord, Chrane, who seemed to have acted on his own by making a thrust at the power and strength of Gorn. Emeralda must have weaved some fantastic tale to convince Chrane to attack. It became evident to us very quickly that the target of the expedition was not the stronghold of the Sages but rather the seat of the lodestone. Emeralda was back to pursuing her obsession and now she solicited the power of the dark side to help in her quest. What twisted plan of betrayal she had in mind for later none could guess but the Sages realized that we had a very large and formidable task to prevent the loss of the lodestone. The Sages quickly mustered a large force which they led into battle with the forces of Chrane on the plains of Gorn. They decided to leave Sapphira, a very powerful, able and talented Sage, and me in the stronghold to protect it. We also had to maintain the force field around the lodestone and the balance against the dark force in the east, which had not shifted with the arrival of Chrane. We surmised that Chrane had acted on his own accord without informing his allies. We hoped to take advantage of this action on his part."

Marlen saw Suzy was somewhat interested but that she was being distracted by his cape. He said, "See the crescent moon on my shoulder. It want you to concentrate on it and as you do you will fly over the battles like a hawk. You will see and hear the events as I tell you the story."

Suzy smiled as she recalled the last time she had listened to and participated in the story of the lodestone. She concentrated on the bright orange crescent moon symbol set against a blue background and suddenly she was soaring above a valley in which a river flowed through a valley of red rocks.

Two armies were advancing towards each other on the opposite sides of the river. Her hawk-like eyes spied Emeralda leading a force of soldiers dressed in black armour and coats. She was riding a brown horse along side a fierce-looking soldier dressed in black armour.

This commander had a helmet topped with a red feather and a visor pulled down over the upper portion of his face. His steed was a black stallion, which was covered with black and silver cloth armour. The horse often pawed the ground viciously and reared angrily, much to the delight of its master who laughed at his antics. The foot soldiers kept well back from this unpredictable beast.

Suzy turned her attention to the other somewhat larger army. Fourteen brightly robed Sages led the group into battle. They were mounted on brown saddles on white horses. Each Sage wore a long sword at his or her side and each carried a wooden staff. The footsoldiers wore white tunics and marched behind the Sages in platoons that were separated by cohorts of horsemen who either carried pikes or bows. Every soldier had a sword.

Suzy watched as the armies approached the Red Falls ford just below the cascading water. The Sages did not hesitate in ordering the army forward and the horsemen of each army met in the river. A fierce fight occurred and the dark army began to fallback. Chrane raised his arm indicating that the footsoldiers should withdraw and they orderly retreated along the path they had traveled. The dark horsemen withdrew from the skirmish and raced after the retreating army.

The cavalry of the Sages secured the far side of the river and waited for the entire army to cross the ford. Suzy could see the enemy moving towards a wooded area out of the valley. She watched as their commander gave orders for them to take up battle positions within the Green Forest.

The Sages now led their force towards the Green Forest. Enemy archers loosed a barrage of arrows but the Advancing soldiers were not caught off guard. They deflected the missiles with their shields and charged into the woods. Suzy watched as the dark army again was forced to retreat before the superior force that was advancing. Chrane and Emeralda ordered the cavalry to the forefront allowing the infantry the chance to escape from the battlefield. The cavalry slowly gave way and then quickly retreated with the footsoldiers.

The Sages used this time to gather the wounded and to heal them of their injuries. Suzy was fascinated that each Sage had the ability to heal wounds. It pleased her to see that the Sages not only healed their soldiers but also the wounded enemies.

She heard shouts coming from the Green Forest from the soldiers who wanted to advance at once on the enemy. She saw the army of the Sages burst from the woods led by the Sages on horseback. All were yelling with great zeal. "Victory is ours! Let's drive the enemy from our land!"

Marlen paused, as he watched Suzy's complete concentration. He drew her attention from the crescent and continued with his account, "Oh, what a dreadful mistake! I know that had I been there, I too would have been caught up in the frenzy of the moment and would have acted in a similar manner."

Suzy returned her gaze to the moon and watched as the Sage army ran down the hill on to the Plain of Elad where the dark army had once again taken up positions. Suzy looked about and realized that the advancing army was moving into a trap. Of course, she could only watch. Chrane and Emeralda ordered their force to attack. From the trees along both sides of the Plain soldiers far outnumbering the Sage army ran into the battle. The Sages tried to order a retreat but the dark army encircled cutting off any way to withdraw. The Sage army drew up in a defensive circle on a small hill as the enemy charged their ranks. Suzy was appalled at the carnage that took place as Chrane continued to attack. The battle continued until nightfall when Chrane ordered his forces to draw back and set up camp.

Suzy watched through the pale moonlight as the enemy set up camp and gathered wood for fires to prepare meals. The Sage encampment remained dark but she saw that the Sages were busy healing fallen soldiers. She also saw a great deal of activity around the edges of the camp but she could not make it out clearly. She saw tents being set up as each soldier pooled their packs for the common good.

60

As the sun rose over the plain, she saw that the Sage army had constructed an earthen wall by digging a ditch around their fortification. They had prepared for an all-out attack and wanted to slow the enemy. Suzy watched as the Sages prepared meals for their soldiers using as little food as possible. They seemed to have a way of stretching the food that was available.

Suzy could see that Chrane and Emeralda were arguing about something so she flew over that camp and overheard their conversations.

"Why are you waiting? We must attack now before any reinforcements arrive." Emeralda said angrily to Chrane, who only shook his head.

"There are no reinforcements unless some are brought from the east. You know that. This group is going nowhere. We can sit here outside their camp and wait for them to surrender," Chrane replied calmly.

"Waiting is for cowards," Emeralda said coldly. "I never expected the great and noble Chrane to sit on his hands while the Sages discover a way to escape. Do not underestimate the power of the Sages—they have been part of the world from the beginning and have repeatedly shown they can crush the forces of the dark."

Chrane studied his companion with care and deep scrutiny. He wondered how loyal she was—Sages did not falter like this one had. However, she had brought him a great deal of valuable information and he was convinced that she would remain true. Yet, he knew she was driven by her own ambitions. "You are in too much of a hurry, sweet Emeralda. The stone will wait for the appropriate time when we can take control of it."

"If we left today we could have it our grasp by the end of next week—then the whole world would bow before us," Emeralda whined.

"We can't leave today because we would have this army after us. We must eliminate it before we proceed," Chrane said frankly. "Until that is accomplished we will continue my way. Is that understood?"

Emeralda frowned and pursed her lips to pout. However, she quickly changed her expression and said soothingly, "Of course, noble Chrane. You are the master of this expedition and I have agreed to help you capture these troublesome Sages. After that, all of Gorn will be ours."

Suzy watched as the supplies dwindled within the Sage camp. Food was being rationed but the men were becoming weaker by the day. Many were disgruntled and complaining was commonplace.

Unhappiness was not confined to the Sage camp. Although Emeralda had pledged her support for Chrane's idea she often spoke of other tactics. "Most noble lord, why do we not leave this group under the command of your captain while we take a small force to retrieve the lodestone?"

"I cannot leave this group. Remember, I persauaded them to follow and leave the main army without receiving the approval of the supreme lord. If I am not here they will mutiny and then the Sages will gain the upper hand," Chrane explained once again.

"The Sage camp is in disarray. They are starving. Why don't you order an attack and wipe them out. Then we could move to more important and precious things," Emeralda offered.

"I want them to suffer before I finish them off. The men may be weakened but it takes much more to defeat a group of Sages," Chrane countered.

"Then give me a small troop of men and I will go for the stone myself," Emeralda said.

Chrane glared at his companion revealing his distrust for her. "No! How many times must I tell you that your time will come?

You will not change my mind with your incessant badgering. Now, leave me alone. I have a campaign to run and you are always interfering."

Emeralda left at once, her face displaying a huge pout as she had again failed to get her way. She went to meet a soldier dressed in the green uniform of a sergeant. She whispered, "I have spoken with your commander. He is willing to send you and seven others with me on a secret mission. I will reward you handsomely if you are very discreet and you keep this quiet. He does not want any foul ups."

"Maybe I should check with my commander. He could advise me on which men would be best to take," the sergeant said, hesitantly.

"Maybe you shouldn't. The noble commander-in-chief wants a very quiet event. If you talk to anyone I am sure he will be most displeased," Emeralda said.

The sergeant blanched at the thought of his supreme commander becoming unhappy with him. He nodded and asked, "When do we go?"

Emeralda smiled, "Tomorrow evening after dark would be a good time. I will leave arrangements in your hands. Remember, your chief expects the best from you."

Suzy watched as Emeralda met the next evening with the small group that her sergeant had assembled. She reminded them of the critical nature of their task before she led them from the camp without being detected by the sentries. Suzy watched as another small group approached from the northwest. She hovered over the group and heard their leader. "Men, this is a very dangerous mission. We will be facing a formidable foe which has our companions completely surrounded. We must somehow get these supplies into the besieged camp. Marlen and Sapphira have told us to wait three days for some disturbance to occur that might distract the enemy long enough for us to rush in. Otherwise, we are to try a dead of night excursion and hope to slip by. Let's do our best." Suzy was certain that mission was doomed.

Suddenly, Suzy heard a commotion in the enemy camp and flew over it. Chrane was pacing back and forth, shouting obscenities at everyone around him. "Who let them go? I thought I had an army of dedicated fighters. Instead, I am surrounded by fools. I can't seem to be able to trust anyone. Nomed, take a force of three hundred soldiers and track Emeralda down. She cannot have gone very far. Take the best trackers with you. I know what to do. Call a general assembly of all our men at once before my tent. I will hand pick your group for you. Go at once."

Nomed scurried away and sound a call to general muster. The enemy soldiers at once headed for the tent of their commander-in-chief. Quickly, they formed up in lines to hear what his eminence had to say.

The small group of soldiers hiding in the trees were surprised by this action. Their leader whispered, "I can hardly believe this. We will wait a few minutes until we can see a way up to the hilltop. Be ready to move quickly."

Chrane shouted over the assembled force. "I need three hundred soldiers to go with Nomed in pursuit of Emeralda and some traitors with her. I want her brought back here. If the soldiers resist, cut them down. I have given my sword of power to Nomed to counter any spells Emeralda might try. As I point to you join with Nomed and begin to depart to catch these traitors."

Chrane walked among the soldiers and pointed to various soldiers who immediately left their rank and followed Nomed who led the designated corps down a path and over a hill.

Suddenly, a soldier near the end of the line shouted, "There is a group of our enemy heading for the hilltop." Chrane yelled, "Archers, shoot them down. We can't let them through." He groaned as he saw that the invaders were well on their way up the hill. The arrows came too late and were short of the mark. The small supply group made it into the encampment without any loss. A shout went up within the enclosure. The dark force groaned and were harangued by Chrane. He was very angry and he kept his soldiers standing in the hot sun for several hours before he sent them back to their posts.

Suzy watched as the Sages prepared meals for the hungry soldiers. The soldiers responded with smiles and songs of praise and thanksgiving. They felt that Chrane would make them pay if he had a chance. Vigilance around the camp was increased in the face of a coming storm.

Nomed and his troop returned within three hours. They had all the soldiers in chains and Emeralda walked behind them. Nomed marched just behind Emeralda, brandishing Chrane's sword of power. Chrane retrieved his sword and took Emeralda by the arm. She did not resist. The rest of the group were marched away towards a stockade designed for criminals. A look of dejection and hopelessness was on each face.

"Did you think I would just let you run off on your own, sweet Emeralda?" Chrane asked in a condescending tone.

"You have been so busy, most noble Chrane. I thought I would help you by completing a mission while you were engaged here", Emeralda replied sweetly.

"Of course, I have been very busy. I should be concentrating on this task but you keep interfering and making my life miserable," Chrane said as he squeezed the Sage's arm.

"Ow! You're hurting me. I can see you are upset but that was never my intention."

"How do I know your intention? You are always insisting on things being done your way. You never co-operate. How am I supposed to get this job done if you keep stealing my attention away?" Chrane shouted.

"Never co-operate! How dare you? I am here with you. I came on my own. I helped you get these Sages into a trap. If it had not been for me you would still be back in the east, groveling at every command your esteemed leader barks," Emeralda said, spitting on the ground.

"I don't need this. I don't need you. I can make decisions and I can win battles," Chrane yelled, his face red with rage. He ran forward, ordering his horse be brought to him. He leapt on to the beast and drew his sword. "Bring my helmet at once. Order the soldiers to prepare for battle." He grabbed the helmet and hastily placed it on his head. He fastened the chin strap.

The camp was astir as bugles blared. Suzy saw that the Sage camp had come to full readiness. Chrane rode to the front of his army and waved his sword to the hill, shouting "Let's run over them. All squadrons attack. Wipe them out."

A bloodthirsty cry went up from the dark army. They charged towards the hill in a frenzy. Emeralda stood where she had been left by Chrane, a small smile on her lips. She murmured, "Fools."

A volley of arrows sliced through the air catching the charging enemy. The mass paused as many went down. A moan went up and then another frenzied shout was released. The enemy charged again. Another volley of arrows took down many more. Suddenly, those nearest the encampment were hit by a blast released by the Sages. They felt their skin burn with extreme heat and they fell back. Another scorching wave rolled over the enemy and now a scream of agony arose. The soldiers turned and ran as blisters formed over exposed skin. Some ran headlong into advancing soldiers taking them down in the confusion. A full scale retreat ensued as the soldiers fled past their commander as he sat immobile on his steed. He remained fixed to that spot with his glare on the Sage camp. He felt Emeralda step up beside him.

"Well done, most noble commander," she said.

"Are you kidding? My soldiers broke like cowards."

"My lord, they did not have a chance. When the Sages called forth heat there are few who can bear it. However, you were brilliant—they can no longer use that weapon against you for one full year. Such is their training and they are bound to it," Emeralda cooed.

Chrane stared at Emeralda and then he grinned. "I was brilliant, wasn't I? My men have seen terror and they will again. I will take time now to grind that camp into misery and I will use this time to pump up my force with fear and desire. They will not fail the next time."

Marlen looked at his young friend and she smiled. "You have seen enough. Just listen to the rest of the story.

Chrane stayed true to his original plan of a prolonged siege and for nine months the Sages held the enemy at bay. However, the rations were exhausted and so were the men."

"When Crane finally did attack, the gallantry of the Sage force was unmatched in history. Three times the enemy were repulsed until Chrane ordered all of his forces into a full scale assault and the hill was overrun. The Sages were captured but only a few soldiers were captured and enslaved. A tunnel was discovered leading away from the hill to a small valley beyond the enemy fortifications. The tunnel had been built during the siege and most of the men had escaped when the first attack came. Even though they were weak with hunger, they managed to flee to freedom.

Chrane was incensed that the army had fled. Chrane had constructed a prison on the site, with twin towers called the Pillars of Gorn. This facility was used to imprison the Sages and the doors were locked with a special key that was hidden away."

Suzy now could not hold back. "Did this Chrane then steal the lodestone with the aid of Emeralda?"

"No, child," continued Marlen, "Emeralda escaped from the enemy camp during the attacks. Locking up the Sages did not destroy their ability to maintain the force field about the stone. Now they could freely concentrate on that task and on the dark force in the east. Sapphira and I were freed from the task of maintaining the force field so we could begin to explore methods of freeing our colleagues from the prison and helping our army in the east."

"What happened to Emeralda? Didn't she get the lodestone?" Suzy asked.

"No, she couldn't capture her prize because the force field prevented her. Obviously, she went into hiding because she now had both Chrane and us looking for her. That's the way it has been for the past fifteen years. I have now come to you because the dark force in the east has begun to grow in strength. I will go into that region to see what is happening and to increase the power of the Sages over that area. I may not be back for a long time and I wanted to alert you to that fact, just in case Emeralda should decide to come your way. Remember your strength and you will be fine. I know the time will come when the Sages are freed from their prison, but until that happens we must keep our resolve to resist and to be alert to the movements of the enemy."

Marlen stood up and stretched. He looked around the little lake and sighed, "I remember days long ago when life was simpler and a place like this could be enjoyed for days and weeks without a care about anything else. There is a trout in that lake that would be a delight to catch." He laughed and Suzy joined him. He placed his hand on her shoulder and said, "Enough of this, little princess. I have to leave on this mission that needs to be done. I have no doubt that you will be fine. Enjoy yourself and keep yourself free of worries."

"Oh, Marlen, I am a bit frightened for you. Please be careful," Suzy said. "I wish I could come with you."

"Indeed!" Marlen chuckled. "We would be quite a team but your time has not yet arrived. I have no doubt that you will come but it will be under very different circumstances than either of us can imagine."

Suzy gave the friendly old gentleman a hug. He turned and walked away. He was soon lost from view by the trees that grew around the dam. Suzy slowly made her way home, her mind filled with adventures and pictures of fame and glory.

-7-

Suzy had gone for a walk after dinner while her mom and dad had their afternoon nap. It seemed strange to her that adults would go for a nap after dinner when she had looked forward for so long for the day when she no longer would have to nap. 'Oh well', she thought, 'parents do some very strange things. I don't think I will ever understand them.' As she walked, she twirled around and around with her hands outstretched. She enjoyed the bright hot sunshine and she was pleased with herself that she had remembered to wear her floppy bonnet that was covered with yellow and red roses and white daisies. She tended to forget instructions. She couldn't explain it but it had seemed like she had been pulled to the closet where her bonnet was kept.

Her twirling brought her to the edge of a pasture covered with bright yellow flowers and to a state of near dizziness so she changed to skipping. Carefully she moved among the flowers so that her feet never landed on any of the petals that waved to her. She missed a mushroom, then a little green toad that was hopping across her path, then avoided a small green pebble. In this way her eyes spied the sparkling cluster among the blossoms. Without hesitating, she reached down and clasped her hand over the shining glitter. Immediately she felt a tingle that slowly spread up her arm and enveloped her entire being. This strange sensation did not frighten her but instead seemed to sharpen her wits. She felt herself spinning and falling to the ground. She did not faint.

She sat up and looked at her treasure. It was a necklace consisting of a delicate little chain, which passed through three sky-blue crystals. Suzy brought the cluster closer to really get a good look at it. The first crystal was a flat octagonal disk. She looked at it carefully and saw a message flash back at her. It did not make any sense but it seemed to say "Call me mint". Her gaze moved to the centre crystal, which was a polyhedron with more sides than she wished to count. It seemed to be full of some sticky substance and as she rubbed her hand over the largest facet, she could feel something ooze on to her palm. Without stopping to consider it might be dangerous Suzy raised her hand to her mouth and licked the sticky deposit. Her eyes filled with delight as she recognized the sweet taste. "Honey!" she exclaimed aloud. She now turned her attention to the remaining spherical gem. Another message beamed back to her. "Three wishes…choose wisely." Carefully she let her gaze move over all the crystals. Whatever material they were made of did not permit any light to pass through them. They appeared mirror-like yet did not cast a reflection.

She instinctively raised the necklace to her neck and fastened the chain so that the jewels rested against the hollow of her neck. Another burst of tingles rippled through her and her vision blurred for the briefest moment. When her eyes cleared, she noticed something strange. In the midst of the field straight ahead she saw a black spot that she had not noticed before. 'That looks like a hole,' she thought and turned her attention to the right. 'What is this?' she wondered, as she noticed another black spot. 'This one is square,' and quickly she glanced back at the first spot.

It was oval in shape. Out of the corner of her left eye she saw something and she spun around to see a triangular-shaped black spot off in the flowers. 'Fascinating,' she thought. She turned back to the first spot and it appeared different now. A quick look at the others and a glance back brought another change. Repeatedly she switched glances and then she realized that the spots were growing larger and getting closer.

"I'll just walk away from them," she said to no one in particular. She set off in the direction that would allow her to pass between the oval and the square but with each step she took, the spots grew larger. She found this most interesting. 'Why am I not frightened by this? Soon they will join together and I will be trapped. I wonder if the triangle is growing.' She turned around, 'Just as I thought. I guess there is no way out except to choose which one I go into. It seems as though that is what is expected of me.' Suzy jumped into the oval without another thought.

She found herself standing in a field of yellow flowers like the one that she had just left. Way off in the distance on the crest of a low hill she saw two pillars rising above a cathedral-like structure—at least that is what it seemed. Nothing else stood out for Suzy so she simply decided to go toward the fingers as she called them. Immediately the pillars took on the shape of two large fingers sticking out of a glove. This change did not frighten or puzzle Suzy. It seemed so natural that whatever she thought, was in fact the way it was going to be.

Off to the right she heard a loud chorus of hissing. A pack of large cats bearing down on her with teeth bared and the hair on their backs standing up. This time a definite sense of dread passed through Suzy because she could tell that she was in danger. She did not panic as her hand felt out her necklace and a feeling of calm swept over her. 'Of course, that's the answer. How silly of me not to think of it sooner.' She took the octagonal crystal and began to rub it over the nearby flowers. She paid little heed to the fact that the menace was bearing down on her quickly. She straightened up, replaced her necklace and set off in the direction of the fingers.

After a while she stopped to look back. She laughed at the sight of the cats slowly moving through her specially prepared flower patch. All the fierceness had left these wild animals and they frolicked with each other, leaping and rubbing against each other. Suzy set off again content in the knowledge that cats cannot resist the scent of catmint.

Suzy bobbed along, her bonnet flapping in the gentle breeze. A loud buzzing disturbed the quietness. A huge swarm of bees had risen off to the left. It had been disturbed by the presence of this intruder in their flower garden. 'Oh my, I do hope I don't get stung.' Suzy's hand crept towards the necklace, 'and of course, why should I?' She removed her necklace and taking the many-faced jewel in hand, she began to rub the larger surface across the flowers as she walked. She kept going straight towards her goal, paying no attention to the rapidly approaching swarm. She restored the necklet to its proper place and continued on her way. This time she did not look back and soon began to climb the hill towards the fingers.

Blocking her way was a deep moat filled with the blackest water she had ever seen. She moved towards her right, which also brought her closer toward her 'fingers.' Suzy found herself on a road that ended at the moat.

She looked at the fingers closely and read the following inscription on each of the pillars—TOWER OF GORN. Immediately they looked like the citadel towers of a castle. On the far side of the water, she noticed a drawbridge but there was no one around to lower it. She grasped the third crystal and murmured, "I wish the drawbridge were lowered."

Suzy stepped back and waited for what she knew would happen. Sure enough, the bridge creaked into action and soon provided a way across the moat. Suzy skipped across the bridge and before her stood a huge door above which was written this message.

WITHIN THESE WALLS ARE IMPRISONED THE SAGES OF GORN. NONE MAY ENTER. ONLY THE KEY OF FREEDOM WILL SET THEM FREE.

Suzy stared at the message, looked at the door and wondered aloud, "I wish I had the key of freedom. I would most certainly let the Sages out." Without her consciously knowing, she had placed her hand on the spherical crystal. She felt it grow warm in her hand so she looked at it. A message flashed before her eyes— 'Chains do not hold the Sages'. She wondered at this and looked around. The massive gate had been lowered using chains which were darkened and rusty. Suzy looked back at the crystal that she held and she noticed that one edge was very sharp. 'I hadn't noticed that earlier.'

Suzy looked up at the chain again and noticed one section was particularly black. It was a very tarnished key tied to the chain with a linen cord. Suzy raised the crystal and used the sharpened edge to cut the cord and free the key. She noticed that where the crystal had rubbed the key it was very shining. 'Of course, the key is made of silver, but it has been tarnished by the weather.' She raised the key to the keyhole in the door and turned. The door swung open and she was greeted by a victory chant from within.

Marching out of the prison were fourteen elders dressed in robes of different hues and shades, covered with signs and symbols. On each head was a pointed hat covered with the same symbols. The Sages looked exactly as they had when she had watched them being captured on this same hilltop. The Sages bowed before Suzy and thanked her for releasing them from the power of Chrane. Suzy looked on with awe as the Sages prepared to leave. The leader turned to Suzy and smiled, "Return to where you came from. Your task is finished for now." The wise troop marched away, across the drawbridge and down the road.

Suzy grasped her pendant, closed her eyes and silently wished to be back home. She opened her eyes to find she was lying in the meadow. There were no black holes anywhere to be seen, but around her neck hung a necklace with three transparent crystals which appeared to be made of glass. Suzy smiled, 'I'll just put you away and keep you as a memory piece. I sure had a great time.'

Suzy skipped on her way back to her house.

-8-

After helping her mom do the dishes and clean up the washroom and the living room, Suzy went outside to have some fun. She played with her pet cat, Puffball, by rolling a ball of yarn towards him. She giggled at the antics of the feline as it would jump in the air and then pounce on the ball. Puffball would put the ball into motion with a stroke of its paw and then stalk it as it moved. If the loose piece made a complete loop through the air as the ball rolled Puffball would leap at the string and attempt to snare it in the air. Suzy knew that if she played this game with the cat for too long it would become bored and walk away so she was careful to stop the activity before that happened.

Suzy then strolled through the yard and observed the Purple Martins as they swooped down from their house high on a pole that Dad had erected. Their house consisted of four distinct rooms and each was the home of a different family. These birds did a lot to reduce the numbers of flies and mosquitoes in the yard, although at times Suzy was sure they were not doing their job. These high fliers would dive and then loop over or swerve to the side in dazzling acrobatic style. She was amused if Puffball walked across the yard because the Martins would be put into a frenzy. They would dive at the cat and then at the last moment swerve, slapping their wing tips together to warn the beast not to come closer. Often Puffball would simply amble across the yard and appear to be completely oblivious to the frantic melee that brewed above him.

Suzy moved on, past the farmyard where the pigs were basking in the sun and the hens scratching at the ground looking for small pebbles, lost seeds or unwary worms or bugs. The horses had chosen to take shelter from the afternoon sun by wandering into the lean-to. Except for the sounds of some birds chirping and the buzz of the occasional honeybee, the yard was still.

"Oh, hum!" Suzy said aloud, "There is not much going on around this place. I think I will go for a short walk and see what I can find."

She left the yard by the tree-lined lane and turned on to the road. No one was in sight in either direction. She began to skip down the road, humming to herself. She slowed as she came to a large rock by the side of the road. Off in the distance she could see a large black bird circling over the field. She was fascinated as the bird would move higher and lower over the terrain in circles of various diameters.

'It almost seems to be looking for something', she thought and then laughed aloud at the idea that a bird might be systematically searching for something that was lost. Suddenly the bird swooped down and landed a short distance from her. Before Suzy could move or even let out a cry of amazement, she saw Emeralda standing before her. She could feel her heart beating rapidly and her breathing became shortened. She had to quickly grapple with a bit of queasiness but she thought to herself. 'Remember what Marlen had to say. He warned me that she could be back, but that she had no way to make me do what she wanted.'

Emeralda smiled at Suzy. "I see you come back to this place

every so often. I've been back here several times looking for something that I have lost. I have never been able to find it...maybe little one, you know where it is?"

"Exactly what are you looking for?" Suzy asked, feeling certain that she knew the answer to her inquiry without asking. She knew that she had to be wary and alert, so as not to give Emeralda any information that might later be used against her.

"The last time I was here with you I was wearing an emerald ear stud. Maybe you remember seeing it while we had some time together and before that intruding old fool interrupted us?"

"I remember you had some type of an ear stud, that's for sure. I did not know that it was an emerald." 'Be careful, Suzy,' she thought, 'don't say too much. I think I will remain quiet about her 'old fool comment'. I don't need to get into an argument with her.'

"Well, I lost it and I think it was around here. I know that although a great deal of time has passed in Gorn not much has happened here. I was really hoping to find it. Usually I can spot it from the air or at least track the trail of anyone who has picked it up. However, this time there is no trace of it, although there were a few times when I have sensed it calling me. It seems to be cloaked by something so that I can not find it."

"What's so important about it?" Suzy asked hoping to put the old lady onto a different path of thinking.

"I need it now because I have this crazy guy who is looking for me. No, it's not Marlen. I mean someone who is really crazy and is capable of the most vicious acts of cruelty that anyone can imagine, probably worse than that. That little gem would help me if we ever come face to face."

"Oh! Emeralda, why don't you just stop pursuing that stupid lodestone. Why don't you come clean? You could be a good person if you really tried. We would all help you if you really wanted to change."

Emeralda cackled as she heard the plea of the young girl. "Easy enough for you to say, little princess. You don't have a mad dark lord pursuing you. Besides, what good is changing? Would it give me the stone? What power and fame would I receive? You don't understand any of this. I would have made you famous but you rejected it. Your goody-goody talk is of no use to me." She laughed again and instantly was gone, circling through the air as she sped away.

'Whew!' thought Suzy, 'that was very close.' She jumped down from the rock and began to walk across the field towards the dam and her favourite spot by the lake. As she approached the little glade, she saw Timmy, a neighbour boy who attended the same school as she did and who competed with her in every subject in class, and every activity on the playground. They were close friends who often got together to play games and share ideas about school. Because they lived very close together and the rest of the kids at school came from the other side of the town Timmy and Suzy often did more things together than with the others. Suzy walked down to the water's edge where Timmy was busy skipping stones across the surface. He was using the technique that the two of them had perfected and was able to get four or five bounces out of every stone before it sank with one final larger splash.

Suzy watched Timmy without talking. After a short time, she reached down, picked up a handful of stones herself, and began to skip rocks during the interval between her companion's tosses. By careful timing, they were able to have a stone touch down just as the last one sank. Not a word was said as they concentrated on their task until the last stone in their hands had been tossed. Then they broke into a fit of giggles and collapsed on the grassy shore. They looked at each other and laughed some more.

Timmy grew silent after a bit and his face took on a more serious appearance. He turned to Suzy and said almost solemnly, "It's not like you to keep secrets from me. I am not sure what all this is about but I worry about you when I see you in the company of strangers, especially the strange lot that have been around here lately."

Suzy did not look up, feeling a bit embarrassed that she had not shared her adventures with her good friend. She wondered how she could tell him that she had been afraid that he might laugh at her wild imagination. She knew he had never done that before but these past events had been like nothing that had ever happened before. She also was very surprised that he had seen anything. She had been so certain that no one had been around. She decided that she had to hear Timmy out and then try to explain what was going on.

"Just a short time ago I saw you with that strange lady that is dressed in black. It's not the first time that she has been around here. I saw her one day at the circus and I also saw you go into her tent. When I stole up to the door to peek inside you were nowhere to be seen. I didn't have a chance to go inside because some guy from the circus told me to scram. He said I had no business snooping on other people. Later on, I was down here by the water when I saw you talking to some white-haired man who was dressed in the strangest cloak. I couldn't make out the designs and I was too far away to hear the conversation but it had your attention for a lot longer than anything I have ever seen before. Just the other day I saw you here with him again and just before he left you gave him a hug, as if he was someone special that was going away for a long time. I tried to follow him but when I got to where he should have come out of the woods, he wasn't there. I never did see where he went."

"No! You wouldn't have either. He travels in ways that we can not understand."

"I know that. I could tell that he was different. That lady this morning just seemed to pop out of the sky and leave the same way, except I did see this large black bird streak away just after you had talked to her. I have uneasy feelings about that one; there is something about her that is puzzling. The old man is different: he seems to be nice and helpful"

"Oh, Timmy, I should have told you about this earlier. You sure do have a good sense about you. I will have to tell you the entire story."

"Just a minute before you do. I left my fishing line over there and I want to check to see if I have caught anything. I'll be right back." Timmy got up and hurried away through the trees. Suzy sat there recalling all the strange things that had been her experiences. She heard a slight rustle in the grass and looked up into the angry eyes of Emeralda.

"I flew away without accomplishing my task, you little imp. You put me off my task, that's what you did. I never did get to ask you about my earring. I'll bet you know something about it. Sure you do and you cannot lie about it either, can you? That's one of the weaknesses some of you people have here. Now where is it?"

"I will not tell you, Emeralda. You intend to use it in your terrible quest of the stone and I will not help you," Suzy said firmly as she gazed into the eyes of the lady.

Emeralda stood still for a long moment; frustrated by this princess that had escaped her grasp and over whom she could not exercise her influence. Anger welled up inside of her as she saw her hopes again being dashed. She reached out to grab at Suzy.

"You little brat. You have my gem and I want it back. If you don't immediately lead me to it I will drag you there by your hair."

"You will do nothing of the kind," interjected a voice from

81

behind. Timmy was standing there with his feet firmly planted on the ground. "You had better not touch Suzy or you will be in serious trouble."

Emeralda stepped back in amazement at this turn of events. This was not supposed to be happening. Her little meeting with Suzy was set up to occur in an opaque shell to keep prying eyes out. She began to scrutinize this young person more carefully and she trembled at the implications. As he stepped forward to stand beside Suzy, Emeralda took another step back. Then in a whiny voice she whispered, "Maybe you can get away from me this time but I will be back and that interfering old fool will be unable to help you the next time. He has been captured by the dark forces near the Eastern Marches and presently is locked away in some castle. I intend to get that ear stud back."

Emeralda turned and began to walk away. Suddenly she turned and stared very long and longingly at Timmy. "You are special, I can tell. I might be back to see you. There is something I can do for you, I know I can." Emeralda lifted off the ground and soared away, a large crow cawing a cacophony that could have been mistaken for laughter.

"Wow! Did you see that? I have never…." Timmy paused as he saw Suzy staring at him. Something about that look told him that, 'Yes, she had seen that before and that there was much more to come.' Timmy threw his hands in the air and said in an exasperated tone, "Come on now, don't look at me like that. First her and now you. Look! I brought my lunch pack with me. Let's sit down here and you can tell me about this."

Suzy sat down beside Timmy and she began to tell the story of her adventures, beginning at the circus and continuing through her two trips to Gorn. She related the visits she had had with Marlen and Emeralda.

She related the last encounter she had had with Marlen when he had come to tell her of a journey that he was going on. Apparently, the dark forces had been successful in establishing an area in the far eastern part of Gorn that had once been a thriving and populated area. However, as the forces of Chrane had ravaged and pillaged the countryside many of the inhabitants had fled while others had been enslaved. Of course, some had willingly gone over to the dark side and were now bolstering the armies of the enemy. Strange stories of a growing darkness had reached the sages but most of it made very little sense. Spies that were sent had either never returned or had been recovered in dreadful states which included death or a mental craze that defied any form of healing that the Sages had at their command. Still, the stories that had come through in small dabs caused a great deal of consternation and the Sages had met and consulted for a long time on what should happen. It was obvious that a first hand look was needed and, after long deliberations, the council had decided that a sage should go into the east to see what was happening. Marlen had volunteered to go alone to avoid being too noticeable and because he had a deep well of experience and wisdom to draw on. The sages had realized that any attempt at mind linking would reveal his mission and so had tried to design a system by which Marlen could leave messages with various living creatures that would carry those messages to Sages who were skilled at deciphering those communications. Marlen had come to Suzy before he had left to let her know what was about to happen. Now Emeralda had told her that Marlen had been captured and locked away. Could she trust such a story? Probably not, yet it raised concern.

After she had finished, the two of them sat in silence on the shore and ate the sandwiches that were in the lunch pack. Suzy followed Timmy back to the fishing line and helped him reel in a nice plump perch. Timmy considered taking it home, but then instead placed his hands in to the water and released it so that it could swim to freedom.

As Suzy watched she realized that here was a special friend that could be called on should she be faced with some very difficult tasks. "I don't know if you can cross into Gorn, Timmy, but I wouldn't be surprised if you can. I don't know what to do, but I am sure that at some point in the near future I am going to have to cross over to find Marlen. He hinted at that before he left. It was like he knew what might happen."

"Suzy, I would like to help. If you ever need me please call and I will be there. You must have had quite a time when you were over there."

"Thank you, Timmy. You are a good friend. Now I think we should head for home. We'll have to get together again to map out some form of plan."

Timmy nodded, and the two of them smiled, as they left the waterside glade and started for home.

-9-

Summer had quickly changed into fall bringing brisk winds and colour changes. Deep verdant greens of grasses and crops were becoming golden yellows and beigy browns. The trees had exchanged their summer apparel of green for their autumn coats of reds and yellows. Some of the leaves had begun to fall to be caught up in the wind and scattered at random. Overhead could be seen the familiar V of the migrating geese and ducks while in the bluffs of aspens could be heard the litany of birds preparing to leave by flocking together. Most garden plants had provided their yields and then had been pulled and fed to the farm animals. The remaining plants showed the signs of having been nipped by the mild frosts of the previous few evenings. The pumpkins were taking on a very golden orange hue while the potato plants were beginning to look like dried sticks. A good deal of garden harvesting would soon need to be accomplished and the yield promised to be an abundant one.

Suzy had spent the morning in the garden helping her mom clear the tomatoes from the vines and now, while her mother busied herself with preserving the ripened fruit, she was in her room tidying and rearranging her furniture. She was busy mentally repeating several Bible verses that she had been assigned as memory work. The passage from Luke 6:35—'But love your enemies, and do good, and lend, expecting nothing in return; and your reward will be great,'—went through her mind over and over as she committed it to memory. She wondered why anyone would be told to love an enemy because of all the evil that they could do to you. She knew that her pastor would take the time in their next class to explain each of these verses and at that time, she would more fully understand the meaning. 'I have come as a light into the world that whoever believes in me may not remain in darkness,' (John 12:46) spread through her consciousness as she switched to another verse.

Presently her attention began to be taken up by the slight sound of bells and chimes that seemed distant and rather muffled. She paused and strained to determine the source of the music. She could not ascertain from where it was coming and she was unable to decide on the melody, although she felt great pleasure at the sound of it. She allowed her attention to move back to the memorization of the verses.

Again, the sound of the chimes wafted across her attentiveness and drew her back to the music that was focusing her mind on its lilting presence. She wondered what could possibly be producing such glorious sounds. She went to the window and opened it. She could not see anything in the yard that would be producing it. She did not feel as much as a hint of a breeze. This was intriguing, she thought, but I must complete this task. She closed the window and pulled the blind. She returned to her bed and sat down with her eyes closed. She concentrated on the verses and became absorbed in the memorization.

Suddenly, the music broke through with an almost painful force and Suzy realized that she had to find out what the source was. The melody had changed and had an almost haunting aspect about it. It gripped at her and commanded her to listen carefully. She realized that it was coming from within her room and slowly she was drawn physically to the top drawer of her dresser. She slowly opened the drawer and was drenched with a burst of harmony unlike all the rest. She felt completely at ease as she carefully slid her secret box from its hiding place. Inside lay the emerald ear stud with its golden chain. Beside it, in a blaze of light and splendor, lay the crystal necklace with each of its gems shining brightly.

Suzy gazed in wonder at the transformation that had taken place. When she had put away the necklace each of the jewels had appeared dull and lifeless, like a piece of glass. Now each shone with a brilliance that dazzled her eyes and held her attention as the song that was being played neared completion in a resounding crescendo. She hesitated to stretch forth her hand and rather let her fingers move slowly over the tiny, delicate chain. She felt reassured and thought briefly of her verses, which further increased her confidence.

Suzy reached into her treasure cove and carefully lifted the necklace from its resting place. Suddenly the gems lost their lustre and appeared as glass. 'Strange,' she thought, 'the last time I was able to carefully look at each and though I did not know the purpose at that time I read a message in each.' Suzy carefully returned the necklace to the box. As soon as she removed her fingers, a blinding radiance burst forth from the gems. 'Oh my, I guess I can't return them. I'll just have to put it on.'

After Suzy had secured the snap, she carefully returned the box to the dresser. She felt as though she was being asked to leave the room and go outside. Without any fear, she went down the stairs and out the door. She looked around and then proceeded down the lane to the road. She looked to her right and saw Timmy hurrying towards her. She smiled and waited for him to draw nearer.

"I came immediately," Timmy volunteered between breaths.

"How did you know?" asked Suzy, realizing that she had not left or sent him a message.

"I heard the most beautiful music that I have ever heard. It drew me from my room and before I realized what was happening I was running down the road towards your place. You have received a message, haven't you?"

"I think so, but I am not sure. Let's walk to the stone bench and I will tell you about it. Obviously you have some part in any adventure that is about to happen, so you may as well know as much as I do," uttered Suzy excitedly.

The two friends ambled off down the road deeply immersed in their conversation and completely oblivious to the presence of a tall figure standing among the pines, all dressed in black. As they talked, they began to pick up speed and were almost in a full run by the time they reached the bench.

Suzy blurted out, "I'll take off the necklace and show you what I saw. I'll set it down on the stone."

"Be very careful," cautioned Timmy.

Suzy very carefully loosened the clasp to the necklace and removed it from her neck. As she set it down she suddenly felt a tug in her fingers and then she was reluctant to let it go. She mustered her will and forced her fingers to relinquish their hold on the gems. As she released the crystals, they began to glow with a reddish throbbing brilliance unlike anything she had seen before. The spherical gem poured forth first a reddish light that changed into a deep purple. The many faceted crystal changed to a bluish light while the octagonal gem emitted a beam of yellow radiance. Both of the youths stood in awe as they watched the light show produced by the necklace. Suzy put out her hand and closed it over the crystals extinguishing the shining. She picked up the necklace and replaced it around her neck.

Almost immediately, Suzy felt a tingling sensation beginning at the hollow of her neck and spreading quickly throughout her entire body, right to the fingertips and the ends of her toes. She shuddered involuntarily as shivers ran up and down her spine. Her gaze became clouded and her eyes began to film over as she began to notice a very bright lumination coming off the pasture beyond the road. Timmy had noticed that Suzy had entered some type of a trance the moment that she had restored the necklace to her neck. He waved his hands in front of her eyes but there had been no reaction. He grabbed her hands to support her and to shake her out of this paralysis. He at once received a massive jolt, like an electrical shock, but he was unable to release her hands. He felt a tingling sensation envelope him and his eyes turned towards the bright glow coming from the meadow beyond the road. He stared hard; the mist over his sight began to clear and he saw a field of brightly and varying coloured flowers laid out before the two of them, like a tapestry of richest tints.

Timmy murmured, "Beautiful" and Suzy gave his hand a quick squeeze, as if to say 'so you see it too.' He turned slowly and directed his comments towards her. "So this is the work of your crystals. It is fantastic. What do you see out there?"

"A living carpet of every hue and shade, so beautiful that it almost takes the breath away."

"Do you see anything else?"

"Why…yes I do. In the midst of the field are some dark spots…"

"Your holes to Gorn are back, aren't they? I see a square one and a triangular one…."

Suzy interrupted him with "I don't see the oval one, the one that I went into in order to save the Sages from the Tower of Gorn."

"Of course it isn't there, Suzy. You used it for the last adventure and that one is over, so the oval hole is gone."

"Do you suppose that we are being beckoned and that is why the holes have appeared?"

"I don't know," whispered Timmy, "this has never happened to me before and I feel just a bit strange. From what you told me it seems likely that the singing from the crystals was a sign meant for you..."

"And for you, Timmy. Don't you see? You would not have heard the crystals if you were not meant to. You must have a particular role to play."

"Yes, I guess that must be true. Let's get on with it."

The two had completely regained their ability to move and they crossed the little depression running along side the roadway. They climbed over the rail fence and entered the brightly lit meadow. They paused and looked at the dark spots that were a short distance in front of them.

Timmy turned to Suzy and asked, "Which one should we enter?"

"I have no idea, but the last time I tried to avoid them and finally just jumped into the closest one."

"Let's try that then," suggested Timmy.

They moved ahead towards the square hole but to their amazement, it retreated before their approach. They looked over at the triangle and could see that it had remained where it was. Timmy took a step towards it and it was still stationary. Suddenly he turned and said quickly, "I just want to check on this." He leaped at the square, which immediately dodged his movement. He tried a feint, by seemingly moving along side the square and then dashing towards it. These attempts proved to be futile, although they did raise a chuckle from Suzy.

"You look silly trying to jump into a hole which isn't there. I think you had better stop that foolhardiness and come over here. It is very obvious what we must do."

"I agree with you," panted a breathless Timmy, "I just had to be sure."

Suzy held up her hand for a moment. "I have no idea what lies on the other side, but I think it is meant for both of us. In Gorn, time can pass very quickly so I think we should enter the hole together so we do not become separated."

Timmy gazed with astonishment at the clear thinking that Suzy had just displayed. He had always known that she was smart but this was something else. He could see no reason to argue with her, so he grabbed her outstretched hand and together they approached the triangle and stepped into it.

-10-

Timmy and Suzy found themselves in the midst of a meadow just like the one they had left behind. It was covered with flowers and surrounded by a low stone fence. Interspersed throughout the meadow were clumps of trees of a variety that neither of the children had seen before. The leaves were large with jagged edges. They had large, almost black veins running across a very dark green surface. Hanging down from each branch were clusters of nuts that were covered with a velvety skin of very fine needles. When the children looked closely at the trees, they discovered another very unusual peculiarity. Each tree had two trunks growing out of the ground that joined above their heads into a single stalk from which the branches then separated. The crown of the tree was perfectly symmetrical in shape.

The children looked about for any sign of activity but they were met with an absolute calm. Nothing was moving and sounds were nonexistent. They wandered through the meadow towards what appeared to be an opening in the stone wall. As they approached it, they noticed it was barred with a large gate made of iron spears. They could tell that it had not been opened for a very long time. This did not bother them since they still had no idea of what to do next. Near the gate they noticed a little roof like structure that could easily have housed a roadside shrine. They were curious and moved closer to discover its purpose.

They could see immediately that it was of very recent construction. The poles supporting the roof were made of freshly cut tree branches while the roof was thatched with the jagged green leaves that they had looked at a little earlier. They walked up to the front of the little building and peered in. On the floor sat two traveling bags, each with a strap so that they could be carried on the back. Once they stepped inside the structure, they discovered that it was indeed very roomy and not at all as small as it had appeared from the outside. They noticed a bench against one wall and sat down. They pulled each bag before themselves and opened the tie top that kept them closed.

A quick flip deposited all of the contents of the first bag at their feet. The collection consisted of a jacket, shirt, and skirt, as well as a bonnet, short knife and a roll bundled in an oily wrap. They stared at the strange collection and were unable to make any sense of the items. They turned to the second bag and dispersed its contents into a separate pile which consisted of a jacket like the other, a shirt, and a pair of pants with the same design as the skirt, a hat with a feather, a bow and quiver of arrows, a knife matching the other and a roll similar to the first.

Suzy reached down and began to open the first bundle that lay on the floor. She carefully unrolled the bundle and saw that it had many pouches on the inside. A careful examination of the contents revealed a cracker-like bread and dried meats and fruits. In the meantime Timmy had opened the other bundle to discover the same network of pouches. As he completed the task of unrolling the bundle, a bright golden object rolled out on to the floor before him.

He reached down and retrieved a golden bracelet. It was

covered with engravings and in the centre was a raised section in the form of five-sided star. The edges of the star were raised and distinct. He ran his fingers over the star and his sense of touch confirmed that the edges were indeed real. He slipped the bracelet on to his left wrist and immediately felt a bout of vertigo sweep over him. He staggered but regained his composure as it passed. He began to feel as fine as he had earlier. Suzy stared at him but returned her attention to the bundles before them. She ran her fingers through the many pouches to make certain there were no hidden treasures that had not been revealed so far. She looked up and gasped.

Timmy had taken on a greenish glow and was becoming transparent. He tended to flutter and continued to grow less distinct. He was saying something but Suzy was unable to hear a sound, except for the faint sigh of a light wind.

Suddenly she cried out. "Its the bracelet. Take it off immediately before you puff away."

She rushed forward and tried to grab Timmy's hand but she simply went through it like a whiff of smoke. Timmy looked at her in astonishment and reached over to his left hand. His right hand did not pass through the left but instead removed the bracelet from his wrist. As he did it the green glow abruptly vanished and Timmy's true essence returned. He pitched forward and Suzy grabbed him before he hit the ground. She carefully laid the unconscious boy to the ground. She rolled up the first bundle, retied it, and made it into a pillow that she placed under Timmy's neck. She noticed that he was breathing normally although he did appear a bit on the pale side.

Presently, Timmy moaned softly and opened his eyes. He stared for a moment at Suzy as though he were trying to recall what had happened and where he was. He tried to sit up quickly but Suzy held him down.

"Not so fast. I don't think you have completely come back to this world."

"What happened? Did I get knocked over the head or something?"

"No, no, nothing quite that dramatic. You fainted."

"Bah!" Timmy snorted incredulously, "I've never fainted in my life."

"Well, snort all you want but it is true. You suddenly pitched over like a falling tree. I caught you so you wouldn't get hurt. Maybe I should have just let you fall. Then how much would you have liked it? I suppose your masculine pride and feelings are a bit ruffled by the fact that you, and not I, have fainted."

"Whoa! Stop for a moment, while this all sinks in," Timmy interjected with a hand raised in a shielding manner. He knew that if Suzy got started on one of her tirades he might have to listen to a repetition of past events for many hours. He shook his head as though he was trying to clear away the remnants of the cobwebs. Half under his breath he mumbled, "Thanks for helping me, but what exactly happened. I remember looking at a bracelet and then things get a bit fuzzy."

"I'll say they did, in more ways than one. You slipped on the bracelet and there must be something about it. Immediately you began to glow with a greenish tinge and then you became wispy, like smoke. All the time you were getting thinner…"

"I remember something hazily. You were shouting and trying to grab my arm but you seemed to keep missing…no that's not right, but it doesn't make any sense…."

"I couldn't grab you. My hand just passed right through you as though you had no substance."

"That's what I remember, but I was afraid to admit it, because it seems like lunacy. Your hand went right through and I expected to feel great pain but instead I just felt astonishment and disbelief. I was talking to you all the time but you didn't answer."

"I couldn't hear anything…no just a minute, there was something, like a hush or a very faint breeze. I remember that distinctly because it seemed like it was trying to tell me something but I guess I wasn't listening very well. I just got very scared when you were vanishing and I needed to tell you about it."

"Well," laughed Timmy, "I had no trouble hearing you, even if I wasn't all there. Your words came through loud and clear and made a great deal of sense. I remember reaching for the bracelet and then…nothing until I woke…came to."

"Is there anything else that you may not be remembering right now? Think hard, I know a bit about these things. They come back with a little effort."

Timmy strained his face and rubbed his fingers into his eyes as he tried to recall everything that had taken place a few moments before. He rocked his upper body from side to side and slowly he began to talk aloud.

"I remember picking up the bracelet and being fascinated by it. It had a special warm glimmer about it but it felt so cold in the palm of my hand. The star seemed to leap out at me and I felt the outline of the figure with my fingers. Thrills and chills raced through me and I felt a great desire to put the bracelet on. As I did it felt so warm on my wrist, but at the same time, I felt my stomach leap and retch. I thought I was going to be sick on the spot. It was as though I had to stand up in front of a large crowd and make a very long speech when I had not prepared for it. As I stroked the star I began to feel at peace and the funny feeling inside me went away."

Suzy straightened up and looked down at her companion for a moment. Then she reached out her hand and said, "Let's take a closer look at that bracelet. Maybe it can tell us something about what's going on around here."

"I know what you mean. We walked in this direction and came upon this shelter. Inside we find these bundles waiting for us, filled with things that seem to be made for the two of us. Doesn't that seem strange to you?"

"Yes, but no. I have become somewhat accustomed to it," Suzy replied. "All of this is here for us, make no mistake about it. In a short time we will either figure it all out or someone will show up with the answers."

Timmy gazed at Suzy with a strange look in his eyes for a moment and then realized what she was talking about. "Yes, I guess you have a bit of experience with this. It just seems weird to me." He reached down and carefully retrieved the bracelet from the ground where it had fallen after he had collapsed. He made certain that he did place his fingers through the bracelet and he did not touch the star. Still, he could feel the power of the bracelet surge through him and he quickly gave it to Suzy.

Suzy stared at the bracelet that lay in the palm of her hand. It did nothing for her. It did not exude any warmth or chill as Timmy had explained. It looked very ordinary and the star had no special appeal to her. She cautiously ran her fingers along the raised edges, expecting a surge of desire but, instead, she felt nothing. She looked up to see Timmy watching her every move, ready almost like a panther to spring on her if she made the wrong move. She allowed her fingers to creep closer towards the bracelet opening and she watched as Timmy tensed.

"I don't think that would be a wise move, do you?" he said almost agonizingly.

Suzy shook her head as if to say that nothing would happen to her. She drove her hand into the bracelet. Nothing!

"See, its just as I thought it would be. This bracelet is not meant for me and so does not have any effect on me."

"Please, Suzy, don't play around with that thing. It may not have any effect right now, but believe me, I know what it did when I put it on. Take it off before something happens."

Suzy glanced over at Timmy and almost laughed at the twisted look on his face. She reached over with her other hand to grasp the bracelet.

"Oh, all right then, I'll take it off, if it will make you feel any better."

She grabbed the bracelet and began to pull on it. As she did so, she felt a sharp pain shoot through her hand and up her arm. The bracelet seemed to turn white hot and her wrist seemed to burn from its touch. She released her hold on the bracelet and screamed in agony. She seized her wrist as her hand became locked in a claw like clutch.

Timmy was on his feet the moment Suzy first began to grimace with pain. He reached out and took hold of her hand in his. At the same time, he wrapped his other arm around her waist and pulled her close. He grabbed the bracelet and slid it off her wrist as she screamed. He felt her go limp as her legs buckled. He steadied her with the arm around her waist and slowly lowered her so that her head rested on the same bundle that he had used earlier.

It was then that he noticed that Suzy's wrist had a very raw, almost blackened band, where the bracelet had rested. The smell of burned flesh was very evident and judging by the moans escaping from Suzy's lips, it was extremely painful. He took her wrist very carefully in his left and then placed his right over it as if to protect it from harm. He felt her relax and very soon her moaning stopped. Her breathing ceased its erratic gulping action and settled into a more regular rhythm. He kept his hands firmly in place over her wound and waited for something to happen.

Suzy's eyes suddenly flickered open for a moment and then seemed to roll upward leaving only the whites to be seen. With a great sigh followed a sudden heaving of her breast she was back and once again looked at Timmy. Her gaze moved quickly to the source of pain and she immediately noticed him holding her hand. A quick tug to release his hold failed to do so and she realized that she did not have the strength to insist. She closed her eyes for a moment and as she did, she remembered what had happened and the excruciating pain that had accompanied it. She now could feel that pain subsiding and she willed herself to relax and to allow the pain to dissipate.

After a brief time she opened her eyes once again and asked, rather quietly, "How long have I been out?"

"Not too long," replied Timmy with a voice filled with warmth, understanding and caring. "I was able to grab you before you hit the deck but I'm afraid we have to find something to put on this terrible burn."

He cautiously raised his right hand to take a better look at the terrible sight that he had beheld earlier. He gasped at the sight before him. Suzy stared at the wrist. Where there had been a mass of burned flesh just minutes earlier there was now a bright pink band of burn scar that throbbed with each heartbeat. Timmy closed his hand over the scar, unable to understand the event that he had just witnessed. Suzy trembled slightly and again closed her eyes. She remembered that Marlen had once said that she had to learn to be patient and she knew that she had been anything but patient. She opened her eyes and looked at her companion who obviously was very shaken by this experience. To think that a few minutes earlier she had been on the verge of ridiculing him and then she had gone off and done something a great deal more foolish. She placed her other hand on top of his.

"Timmy, about what I said earlier..."

"No, forget it. We both need to slow down and think things through."

"Still, I really was out of line and I appreciate you being here."

"Maybe we should look through this bundle for something to fix up your wrist," Timmy said to change the topic. He removed his hands from hers and turned to look through the collection of materials spread out before them. His newfound attention was disturbed by a quick yelp from Suzy and he directed his concentration back to her. She was slowly rotating her left hand in the palm of her right as she stared at the wrist that had been severely burned. Timmy could not believe what he was seeing, though it was right there in front of his eyes. The terrible burn that had only a short time ago appeared as a bright pink scar now was a faint light pinkish white band that circled her arm. The scorch marks that had been present the entire length of the hand after the removal of the bracelet were completely gone. Timmy took Suzy's left hand and raised it up to his face to better observe the scar.

"How does it feel?" He asked.

"There is no pain. Just a little tingling."

"A tingling, that's all. This is weird, totally weird."

"How did you do it?"

"What do you mean?" Timmy asked.

"Before I passed out there was extreme pain coming from my wrist. The bracelet was glowing white-hot and burning my flesh. You grabbed my hand and pulled it off. How? I don't know what happened next but when I came to my wrist was already better. What did you do?"

Timmy just shrugged his shoulders, "I didn't do anything. I just grabbed the wrist and pulled it off."

"Let me see your hands."

Suzy took his hands and turned them over. There was nothing different about them.

Suzy said excitedly, "They are not burned. Did you not feel any pain?"

Timmy shook his head and then continued, "I pulled off the bracelet and held you from falling. I put you down and held your hand between mine. I looked at the burn once early on and it was a horrible mess. I couldn't think of anything to do except to hold your hand to shield it from harm. You seemed to relax and breathe more easily. I don't understand a bit of it."

"Nor I," replied Suzy. She rolled her hand over again and then looked at Timmy's again. Presently she dropped her hands to her sides and said matter of factly, "Well so much for that. Let's look through the bundles and see what else there is."

The two of them enthusiastically began to investigate the pouches. They quickly forgot about the strange episode and unpleasant experience. However, their search was short lived since there really wasn't much in the pouches to catch their fancy. They stood up and looked over the collection of items that were on the floor before them. Timmy reached down and picked up the clothes.

"I believe these are meant for us to wear. I don't now why, but somehow I suspect that if we don't put them on soon we will not be getting on our way."

"My thoughts exactly," responded Suzy as she looked around the shelter. Her eyes spotted a couple of screens like those used in clothing stores for trying on new garments. "Why don't we put on our outfits in those change areas?"

"A great idea!" exclaimed Timmy and they made their way into the two screened off areas.

-11-

In a short time the two of them made their way back into the centre of the shelter dressed in their new outfits and carrying their old clothing over their arm. They sat down by the bundle and spied a large pocket into which they placed their carefully folded clothes. They picked up the bundle and rolled it up, securing it by tying the leather straps together. They placed the short knife in a special pouch made for the purpose inside their jackets. Timmy lifted the quiver after placing the bow into it and slid his head through the opening that the strap made, allowing the pack to fit up against his back where it felt very comfortable. They tied the bundle to their waists so that it rested against their lower backs. They stood back and inspected each other, before bursting into laughter.

"We look like we are ready to go on a long safari or something," chuckled Suzy.

Timmy was about to reply when he spotted the bracelet lying in the dust on the floor of the shelter. He hesitated and then carefully picked it up, bracing himself for the charge of magnetism that had spread through him earlier. Sure enough, another surge flooded him but he had prepared himself for it and its intensity was short lived. He turned to Suzy and said, "I'm at a loss as to what I should do with this. I don't think I can leave it behind but I can not wear it." He looked down at it for a moment and returned his gaze to Suzy. He nearly did a double take when a tall blue-robed woman stepped into view, smiled at him, and commented, "You indeed are going on a trip and it looks like you have prepared yourselves by dressing well."

Suzy twirled around at the sound of the voice and stood spellbound at the sight of this visitor. She looked very carefully at the smiling face that was filled with warmth. It had only a few tiny wrinkles and the eyes sparkled with the most royal of blue. The blond hair was combed back and disappeared into her shawl. In her left ear she wore a silver stud, which was crowned with a bright, almost transparent, sapphire.

"Oh! Excuse me for staring," she blurted out, "you must be Sapphira. Marlen has spoken a great deal about you but I never expected to meet you."

Sapphira looked about and said, "Oh really? Has Marlen been spreading lies about me, like he always does?"

"Oh no!" Suzy exclaimed. "He has had nothing but kind things to say about you.... You sure are beautiful."

Sapphira laughed, "You do have a way of bluntly stating a compliment. Thank you anyway. You must be Suzy. I have heard so much about you and now I can see there is more here than meets the eye." The tall woman held out her hand to Suzy who took it gently in her own. Then Sapphira continued, "I haven't had the honour of meeting your friend and companion on this adventure." She held out her hand to Timmy.

Timmy took her hand and bowed slightly. Suzy stepped forward to introduce her friend. "This is my friend, Timmy. He has shown some very unusual strength and insight and has volunteered to come on this venture."

Sapphira held his hand for a moment and then turned it over in hers. She reached out, grabbed the other hand, and turned them palms up. She studied them for a moment and then remarked, "You have the hands of a healer. They have such strength and power in them. It seems you have used them just recently to help someone."

Timmy and Suzy stood there mesmerized by this amazing woman. They looked at each other, then at his hands, and back to her.

Suzy spoke up, "How can you tell?"

"His hands emit an aura that has a few breaks in it. This indicates that they have been at work."

Timmy interrupted, "You mean that just by holding my hands you can tell so much. What type of person are you anyway? I'm not meaning to be rude but I find all of this so very strange."

Sapphira smiled and then became very serious. "No, its not rude. I have been a little impolite in not introducing myself. As Suzy has said, I am Sapphira, a very dear friend of Marlen. We are both members of the Council of Sages, a group that Suzy here had the privilege of releasing from the Towers of Gorn and the wicked power of Chrane. Marlen and I were fortunate not to be included in the capture so this is the very first time that I have had the opportunity to meet Suzy. You have some very strong and hidden powers, Timmy, that will become evident as time passes. One of these powers is that of healing and as a Sage who has studied for a long time, I can recognize its presence. However, I also detect the presence of another force in this vicinity and I can feel some of its field coming from your hands. I can not tell what it is but it has some unknown quality about it."

Timmy looked at his hands again and then realized that he no longer had the bracelet that he was so concerned about earlier. He looked about and then spied it lying on the floor. He surmised that in the excitement of meeting this wonderful person he had let it fall from his hands. He reached down and mentally prepared for the invasion of his privacy that he knew was about to occur. As his hands closed over the bracelet he saw waves of deep blue and violet light wash across his mind. He willed them out of existence and then straightened up. Sapphira reached out and placed her hand under his elbow to steady him. Her face had taken on a very grave appearance.

"Carefully," she cautioned, "it's a tool of Chrane. I have absolutely no idea how it got here but it means that somehow Chrane has realized that you would be here and left that bracelet. I think that you probably have a story to tell me but first let me sit down. I think we could all use a little snack and a cold drink. I have some light biscuits and rose petal tea, so please join me. Then you can tell me all that has happened so far."

The three of them set up a table and found some stumps that served as stools. Sapphira laid out a lunch and set up three mugs that she found in the shelter. The children were amazed that all they needed was right at hand in their environment. Suzy understood better than Timmy did since she had been in Gorn a few times and had experienced that aspect of the place previously. They sat down and while they had their lunch, the two children told of the incident with the bracelet, each interrupting the other to fill in some detail that the other seemed to be missing. Through it all Sapphira sat quietly listening and did not interrupt any of the conversation. As they were summing up Timmy leaned ahead and, almost in a whisper, murmured, "You sure are a good listener. You have so much patience. My parents would have yelled at us for talking so fast and for interrupting each other. They would have said that they could not understand a word that we had said."

Sapphira chuckled, "Well, maybe your parents have some

sense after all. Perhaps you have just provided a little lesson for yourselves."

The two children stopped and gaped at the woman. They looked at each other and then turned a deep red as they realized what they had been doing. Suzy spoke up.

"Marlen warned me that I talk too much and that I just let my mouth run on so, without letting my brain do anything. I'm so sorry, Sapphira."

"Me too," mumbled Timmy.

Sapphira reached out and touched each on the head, making them feel more comfortable in her midst, not ill at ease or under a critical eye. She needed to find out more.

"Suzy, I need to look at your hand where the burn occurred."

Suzy raised her left hand so that Sapphira could get a better view. They saw the pink had now left the wound and the distinct white of a scar was beginning to fade. Sapphira looked over the entire wound and then allowed Suzy to reclaim control of her hand.

She turned to Timmy and said with a smile. "Well, young man, I said earlier that you had the hands of a healer and what a healer you are. All you did was hold a severely burned hand between your hands and look at what has happened. Normally a burn like that takes months to recover, if in fact it does. Here in less than a few hours it is well on its way to being fully restored."

Timmy turned to Sapphira and rested his hands on hers. "I want to know exactly what has happened here. What is that bracelet? I had it on and nothing happened, but look at the damage it inflicted on poor Suzy."

"You have right to be bewildered. That is a bracelet of Chrane, as I said earlier, and it appears Chrane has put some mysterious power in that band. You seem to have some power over it in that it does not harm you. Perhaps, it is because you have healing hands, I do not know. However, it does have some power over you since you are deeply affected by it. It seems to make you become vapourous and quite likely will make you vanish. However, that takes time so you can't just vanish all at once. I think you should hold back from trying that until some need arises—then be careful that you can find the band because you could be invisible to yourself as well."

"Can't he just leave the bracelet here?" asked Suzy.

"I doubt that very much. I believe now that he has worn it that it has some hold over him. He would be forced to return for it and that would simply delay our departure."

"I don't know what to do with it," said Timmy, "I can't wear it on my wrist and if I touch it with my hands I feel funny."

"Why not try a leather strap through it and wear it around your neck?" volunteered Suzy.

"We can try it," supported Sapphira.

Timmy just shook his head as if he already thought this was a poor idea. A piece of leather was found and Sapphira began to thread it through the band. Immediately the leather began to smoke and momentary burst into flame. Sapphira recovered as much of the strap as she could. Timmy ran his hands through his hair and spoke up.

"Maybe we should have a leather pouch in which to place the band and then use the straps to hang it around my neck."

Both of his friends thought this was a good idea and shortly a pouch was found, fitted with the bracelet and placed around Timmy's neck.

Then the three companions tidied up their shelter and put the packs in place on their backs. They took one last look at their shelter and exited to the gate that stood before them. Sapphira approached the rusty lock and taking her staff she struck the lock with the end. Sparks and a bluish flame erupted from the collision and the lock sprang open. Sapphira removed it and let the old chain fall free. Then she pushed open the gate and the trio passed through into the fields beyond.

-12-

Emeralda had watched as the two young people had hurried by on the road, oblivious to her presence. She had followed quietly and at a distance, so as to remain undetected. She had watched as the two stepped through an unusual portal and vanish from sight. She knew that Suzy and Timmy had slipped into Gorn so she approached the area where they had made the transition. She was surprised that she felt a strong resistance to her movement. She discovered that she was unable to move into the area where Timmy and Suzy had held hands and made the jump into Gorn. No matter which direction she took to reach that spot she just could not step closer. A barring spell had some how been activated to keep her from following the travellers.

She marvelled that these two would have access to such a powerful spell. 'So,' she thought, 'these two have some very powerful magic under their control. They will need to be watched very closely. However, right now there is nothing left here to do.'

Emeralda then returned to Suzy's yard. Emeralda had earlier sensed the presence of her missing earstud. She was certain that Suzy had hidden it away and that it had to be nearby. Now that Suzy was in Gorn Emeralda felt she could search for the earstud without interference. However, as she quietly slipped around the yard the presence that had lured her ceased to call to her. In fact, Emeralda felt the presence of another force blocking her attempts to reconnect with the earlier sensation. The force was intangible and inexplicable, yet it repelled her movements and attempts to locate the gem. She made her way out of the yard and stood within the shadows of the shelterbelt.

She struggled within herself about these two failures that had come so closely together. She hardly noticed a troop of young people come down the road and past the spot where she was hidden. The group consisted of young girls wearing brown shirts,shorts, and a yellow scarf and of young boys wearing tan khaki shirts, shorts and a blue scarf, of older boys in a tan khaki uniform with blue scarves. Accompanying the group of children were three adults, two men wearing uniforms similar to the older boys and a woman wearing a striped shirt and a navy blue skirt. Emeralda was immediately intrigued by the order displayed by the group as they marched down the road. Moreover, as she counted the number in the troop she was amazed that there were twenty two young people assembled together. This was an amazingly large number of young people, something that was extremely rare in Gorn. The number of young people in Gorn was very low, yet here Emeralda was witnessing a larger group than she had seen in hundreds of years. Indeed, this was more than she had seen when Gorn was young when more youth had lived. She was so fascinated that she began to follow the troop at some distance. She suddenly realized what she was doing. She quickly looked around to make certain no one else was about. She did feel fairly certain that her presence was masked and that no one would have been able to see her. Still she was a bit apprehensive since the incident with Timmy when he had seen her talking to Suzy. She was uncertain whether there might be others who would see her. She quickly changed into a crow and glided overhead, keeping a close watch on the progress of this group.

The troop turned off the main road on to a narrow lane. They made their way up a slight rise to a fenced compound on the crown of the hill where there grew three large fir trees. Around the inside of the fence grew a well-groomed hedge. One of the men opened a wrought iron gate so all the members could pass through.

Emeralda flew over and perched herself on one of the trees, watching the group assemble around a mound of freshly piled earth. Emeralda was baffled at the very quiet children who seemed to display great sadness. She noticed that a few were even crying. 'What kind of place is this,' she wondered and looked around to get a better idea. There were stone monuments, most of which were in the shape of a cross. She noticed writing on the monuments, etched or chiseled into the stone. She recognised these to be names. Below each were a set of numbers, separated by a dash. She suddenly realized this must be the resting place of persons who had lost their lives. She looked more carefully at the small marker by the new mound of earth. She was shocked because the numbers indicated that this was the burial mound for a child. This was a shock since she had seldom heard of such a thing in Gorn. Children grew into adulthood. Death was a rare occurence since the Sages held the power to heal injuries and wounds so that life continued uninterrupted. Her gaze sought out other monuments and she was deeply moved by the number of young people who no longer lived.

The leader of the troop began to speak. "Dear friends, we are here to say goodbye to our dear friend, Johnny, who served as a faithful member of our pack. He was a comrade and a classmate. We do not know why that dread disease came to him, but we all saw how valiantly he faced that foe. We can only hope to learn from his example of bravery so that we too can face all trials with his resolve. Goodbye Johnny"

The troop leader stood at attention and saluted. Every member did the same and then placed a small flower on the mound of earth. The leader ushered his troop out of the cemetary and closed the gate. They departed in silence. Emeralda flew down from the tree and changed her form. She was deeply disturbed by what she had just witnessed and learned. She had experienced death before, the most recent being that of Ebony, her longtime partner and in latter years her burden. But this place revealed a new aspect that she had never known before. For a brief moment this hardened Sage felt a a deep remorse and a sense of unfairness that such a thing should happen to someone so young.

Suddenly she realized that the day was quickly passing. She knew her time here was being wasted. She had other tasks to which she had to attend. Somewhere there was a stone that was calling her. She had to go. She stepped towards the fence and vanished, leaving the enclosure to the silence of the ages as she returned to her homeland.

-13-

The day was miserable even though the rain had stopped falling about an hour before. The trio were not getting any drier because a heavy mist had settled in. Their clothes were soaked and the damp material was beginning to rub their flesh raw, adding to the general discomfort and irritability of the younger members of the group. Yet, Sapphira continued to trudge on splashing through puddles of water and mud. Suzy had wanted on several occasions to call out to her to get a rest but had lost her nerve. Instead, she followed close behind and stared downward. She had watched as Sapphira's long gown had become soaked from the hemline up. It had then become caked with mud and filled with burrs and thorns. Suzy knew that her own clothing must be covered in mud but she did not bother to look. She also did not look back to see where Timmy was because she could hear his plodding along just behind her. She had tried to look back once but had nearly tripped in a hole. She had twisted her ankle slightly and every once in a while it sent a painful reminder to her. When she did sneak a peek around her she could not see anything distinctively because of the rain at first and now because of this almost opaque mist.

Timmy was carefully picking out the places to step but it did not help stop the soaking that he was forced to endure. He had no idea where they were or where they were going. He had given up trying to pick out landmarks because there were none to be seen. He had seen Suzy slip in that depression and then come up limping. He was amazed at her perseverance, as she had continued to march on. He could tell that she was hurting and that every so often she aggravated the injury. Once in a while the water that accumulated in the ridge of his hat would spill out and run down his neck. All he could do was shrug it off and keep up. He wanted so badly to call out to Sapphira for a rest but he knew she was in charge. It was a good thing he was not leading because he had no idea where they were going.

Suddenly Sapphira stopped and the two children nearly ran over her. They stepped to the side to see that they had come to another gate like the one that they had passed through three days earlier as they entered this meadow. This time it did not have a lock or a chain and so with a push Sapphira made an opening and they passed through. Ahead of them, looming out of the mist was a rock face covered with small shrubs. Sapphira led them along a ledge to a crevice in the rock. Passing through that gap they entered a semi-darkened cave. Here it felt dry. In a few minutes they gathered up the dry branches that were strewn about the place. Sapphira bent over the small pile that had been built up and struck it with her staff. Immediately the branches burst into flame, illuminating the cave.

The walls were covered with paintings of animals and hunters. The colours were very bright and vivid. The children stared at the sight for a few moments until Sapphira called to them. She wanted to go back outside to find some logs before their fire burned away. They followed her out and soon were returning with some bigger pieces of timber that were very damp.

Sapphira indicated that they should be placed near the fire. "We need to dry out the wood as quickly as we can so that we can use it to keep the fire going"

The children nodded since this made sense and went back outside to retrieve more wood. After about four trips Sapphira indicated that they had enough and that it was time to rest. At this point she told them to remove the damp clothes and put on their dry garments for the time being. Each found a secluded part of the cave to change. When the young people returned to the fire they saw that Sapphira had removed her long blue gown and replaced it with a red and blue jump suit. She no longer seemed as commanding as she had earlier. They spread out their clothes to dry and then sat down to a meal of the crackers and dried meat that they had carried in their packs. Sapphira had placed a small kettle on the fire filled with water that she had scooped out of a rock basin just outside the cave. When it was boiling she threw in a handful of dried leaves and berries that she carried in her pack. The aroma instantly filled the cave and made the children nearly swoon with desire for some of the tea that was being prepared.

They drank the tea slowly, watching the fire as it slowed and shrank back to a small flame and a large pile of bright red-orange coals. No one said anything because of fatigue. Sapphira rose to get a few more pieces of wood, which she placed on the fire. The coals glowed brightly and slowly began to spread to the damp logs. Sapphira found a spot to sit across from the children.

"It is time that you learned more of what is happening. For the past three days you have patiently followed my every step and, though I could sense your frustration and anxiety, you never once complained. Today, Suzy, you hurt yourself and never murmured your discomfort out loud. I commend the two of you and I now realize that choosing you for this mission was the correct decision. Before proceeding we should have a closer look at that ankle.

Suzy felt a bit embarrassed that everyone should want to look at something she had kept to herself. She peeled back her sock to reveal a swollen and bruised joint. Sapphira touched it and Suzy jumped. "Just a reflex", she said as an excuse.

"No, little one. That must be painful and even though you are brave it would be foolish to continue this way. You have some hard roads to travel and you can not hope to make it on an injury like that."

Suzy was about to object but Sapphira held up her hand and continued, "Fortunately, there does not have to be any delay because we have Timmy and he can put his hands to work to heal that sprain."

Timmy got up immediately. "Why didn't I think of that sooner?"

Sapphira said in his defense, "You have just uncovered this strength and it is not a familiar part of you. It is very logical to forget that you have healing hands, especially since that power is only exemplified in Gorn."

Timmy placed his hands around Suzy's ankle and immediately she began to feel the pain and pressure begin to subside. She was relieved that she would be able to carry on with the mission.

Sapphira returned to her place opposite the two of them and sat down. The glow of the flames reflected off her face so that she seemed to illuminate the entire cave.

"Marlen was captured by the dark force…"

"Yes, we know. Emeralda told us that," interrupted Suzy.

"Oh, did she?" continued Sapphira. "So you have had a meeting with her. I'm sure she was her most pleasant self as always."

Suzy was quick to reply, "I know that Emeralda is a wicked

person who has only one thought in mind, but she can't really be blamed for the way she is. I wish that there was some way to get through to her since I feel that deep down she must be a very kind person."

"Suzy," Sapphira continued, "you are a very remarkable young girl. Marlen once said that your talents are hidden and that your special gifts have not yet been displayed. You are describing an Emeralda from a long time ago when she truly was a lovely person. I know…she is my sister and I too wish that I had her back the way she was…" Sapphira looked away for a moment as her face displayed a deep and terrible hurt from the past. A single tear formed and ran slowly down her left cheek. She reached up and dabbed it away before continuing. "But times have changed and we have to be on our constant guard because evil has taken her over."

Suzy placed her hand over her mouth and burst out, "See I did it again. I will never learn to keep my mouth shut. I am so sorry, Sapphira, but I did not know. Why does this happen so often?"

"Hush, little one. Of course, you didn't know. It's just something with which we must live. Let's get on with what needs to be done, but first how is our healer coming along?" Sapphira walked to where Timmy sat holding Suzy's ankle. He released it and everyone was astonished at the change that had taken place. The swelling was gone and the bruising had disappeared. Suzy tried twisting and turning her foot and then giggled because it no longer had any pain. Sapphira smiled and returned to her place. Suzy pulled her sock back over her healed foot.

"Marlen left the Council to go into the east so that he could be closer to the Dark forces. He had hoped to monitor the buildup of strength that was taking place and to observe the movements of that great army as they prepared for another assault on the forces of Gorn. He cunningly made his way past several vanguard lines and was very close to the camps of the Dark High Command. He was mind linked with me and relayed some information about the size and disposition of the forces. However, that mindlink was also the cause of his downfall. Why we did not think about it before, I don't know, but it was very foolish of us not to have anticipated the problem. I told you that Emeralda is my sister; well, she is more than that. She is my twin. Don't look so shocked!! We shared our mother's womb and were born within minutes of each other. We had developed a very close relationship from before our birth and that special link has never been severed. After Emeralda encountered the lodestone and changed we believed the bond ended. Emeralda used her powers to deceive and secretly use those around her. She must have tapped into the mindlink with Marlen and then relayed that information to Chrane. His forces waylaid and captured Marlen. She had to do something to return to the good graces of that evil tyrant and now no doubt she is enjoying the fruits of that deceitful treachery."

"I am not so certain of that," interjected Suzy. "The last time Emeralda came she said that Marlen had been captured but also that she was being pursued by some crazy and evil person. I didn't know what she was talking about but I have no doubt now that she was referring to Chrane."

"Perhaps she is beginning to taste some of her own medicine. She has always thought that she could outmaneuver and manipulate everyone that she dealt with. Yet now this Chrane is using her and he obviously still wants her in order to reach the lodestone. This is quite a development and one that needs some attention very soon. I had better continue with the story concerning Marlen. He was captured and Chrane placed him in a castle that was especially constructed for him. Chrane knows that Marlen is an important part in the defense of Gorn and he has set up a terrifying field about him. We no longer can mindlink with him and when we try, we are repulsed by an evil thrust that sears the mind. We have an idea where the castle is but no one has seen it. In that region of Gorn a deep darkness has fallen through which no one can travel."

"Where exactly is this place?" asked Timmy.

"We are very near to where the darkness starts. Since it came into being this area has been soaked by the constant deluge of rain that we have been walking through."

Timmy ventured another question, "How exactly will we get through this darkness to help Marlen?"

"That has yet to be revealed to us, or should I say, to the two of you. My role in this adventure was to guide you to the edge of the darkness and then you are to carry on the mission. I had thought that perhaps I was to play some role in that but now I know differently. Your revelation about Emeralda and her fleeing from Chrane makes it imperative that I return to inform the Council of the situation. Somehow the right procedure will be made known to you or you will somehow make the necessary decisions. We know the power that each of you possesses will lead you through this trial."

"Oh!" sighed Suzy, "I know that this is often the way it is in Gorn, but I wish that we had a better idea of what lay ahead and what to expect."

"That is a characteristic of your world, not of Gorn. Here we know that the future unfolds before us and we have to be ready. It's much like reaching the edge of a river and if you are ready and observant then you can cross easily by stepping from stone to stone," remarked Sapphira.

"What happens if you are not ready?" inquired Timmy.

"Well, you step where you think the rocks are and if you are fortunate you make it across the river soaked but still able to go on. Or perhaps someone helps you across but you are still soaked. Or you get across but are injured and then life is adjusted to that situation."

Both of the children looked at Sapphira and waited for her to continue because she had, they felt, not described every alternative. After a moment of silence, they realized that this part of the conversation had come to an end so Suzy spoke up.

"What should we do now?"

"We should all get a good sleep tonight because the way ahead of us is long and filled with a great deal of uncertainty. We will require all the strength we can muster."

Sapphira rose and moved to put a few more logs on the fire so that the heat would last through the night. The children prepared for sleep by gathering some of the dry moss that was available in the cave and making a cushion on which they spread their blankets. After a moment of prayer they were soon fast asleep. Sapphira watched as they dropped off. She settled into her blankets for some rest. She knew that so much had happened that required deep contemplation. Sleep would likely be very short this night.

-14-

Timmy stirred and turned over in his blanket. He suddenly became aware that the air in the cave was becoming quite chilly so he opened his eyes to look about. The fire had gone down to very faint embers. He looked around in the near darkness and saw that Suzy was curled up in her blankets and sound asleep. He turned his head and noticed that Sapphira and her bedroll were missing. He sat up abruptly with the knowledge that they were now on their own. He crawled out quietly and found dry wood, which he placed on the embers. As the fire began to replenish itself on the new fuel he found his dried clothing and discovered that they were clean and spotless. He looked at Suzy's and could see that they were the same. 'Sapphira,' he thought to himself, 'I don't know how you do it but you are truly a most remarkable person. I only wish that you could have stayed to help us.' As he dressed himself he spotted a piece of paper. He picked it up and read.

Dear children, I had to leave at once and could not bring myself to waken you from such a deep sleep. Besides, it would have just delayed my parting. I have received word that my presence is needed at once back at the Council and I must use all my powers to return as quickly as possible. I know that you might be apprehensive about what lies ahead, but rely on your strength, your training and each other and you will be successful. Remember, that in the darkness everything is invisible and that the way to overcome the darkness is to bring forth the light. Until we meet again, I am your friend and servant, Sapphira.

Timmy put the paper down and checked the fire again. He then ate some cracker-bread and dried fruit. He saw that Sapphira had left her kettle and poured some of the tea for a drink at this light breakfast. He had noticed the food he had just eaten satisfied his hunger. Furthermore, he remembered that it had given him the energy and strength to go on for long periods of time between meals whenever he had previously eaten it. After he had finished his drink, he stood up and went back to the note. He read it over again and wondered what Sapphira meant by "Remember that in the darkness everything is invisible and that the way to overcome the darkness is to bring forth the light." He found a pencil and jotted down a message on the flip side of Sapphira's note for Suzy. Then, he went to the entrance of the cave and peered out. The rain was not falling and the mist had almost completely lifted. He checked around so that no one saw him leave the cave. Timmy quickly scrambled over the rocks to a path that he noticed the night before when they had been gathering the wood.

He did not have a plan except to check out the path before returning to the cave to tell Suzy about it. He also wanted to see how far ahead the veil of darkness as described by Sapphira the evening before was. After that they could start to make some definite plans about their next course of action. The path was rocky so Timmy knew he would not be leaving any trace from where he had come. He could see that the path made its way between two very high rocks and that the passage was very narrow. Timmy approached the towering sentinels cautiously and then looked beyond them into another meadow. However, he could only see a short distance since a wall of darkness descended on this meadow like a huge curtain across a stage. Timmy was fascinated with the finality of the scene. He had no other way to describe it since he had never seen anything like it before. He looked about and after ascertaining that he was alone in this place moved down to the edge of the darkness. He tried to peer into the murk but it was impossible to see anything. He walked along its edge to discover a hole or a window, but he soon decided there would not be one. Every once and awhile he noticed a small brook either flowing into or out of the darkness. It made him realize that this was not a wall but simply a transition from lightness into darkness. He turned and faced the void for a moment as he thought about his next move.

He then stepped ahead and entered the murk. The absolute darkness blinded him and he realized how one who had lost his sight must feel. He then took two steps back and was forced to close his eyes at the absolute brightness of the area that was not covered by the dark.

Suddenly, he heard the sound of footsteps coming and though he looked around he could not see the source. Then he realized what Sapphira had meant by "in the darkness everything is invisible." He had been unable to see when he had entered the darkness and now something was coming his way from the darkness. He listened carefully and he could hear the sound of water splashing with each footstep. 'Of course,' he thought, 'they are following the little brook so as not to get lost in the darkness. So, they can not see in the darkness either.' Timmy looked around to find a place to hide but he could not find anywhere to go. He could hear that the steps were getting closer and closer. He knew he had only one place to go. He decided to step back into the dark. He would wait for whoever it was to pass. He took two steps into the darkness and waited.

Presently, he heard loud cursing as the travelers stepped into the light. They were almost in agony as they tried to adjust to the brightness that had flooded over them. He heard one of them bellowing, "I hate this. We always have to do this stupid patrol and there is no way to prepare for this transition. What for, I ask you? There's nothing ever out here. This will just be another wasted trip."

"Stop your griping, Blog. You never stop. Do want Chrane to know that you have been questioning his orders? You think you're so brave speaking like you do. Well, when he is finished you won't have any guts left."

"And I suppose you would tell."

"No but these rocks seem to have ears."

Suddenly another voice piped in, "Over here, I see some tracks."

Timmy realized how close that voice had been to where he stood. He decided to take three more steps into the dark. However, after his second he abruptly ran into something. This frightened him greatly until he felt about and realized it was a tree. He moved around it and waited. 'Boy, that was invisible.' he mused to himself. He could clearly hear the voices near where he had entered.

"Whatever or whoever was here went into the darkness right here."

Timmy heard a raucous laughter come from the one that he had heard called Blog. "Well, Vinky, you have good eyes to see those tracks. Whoever made them sure is a fool. There is no path here and in that mess you can easily fall into a hole and be lost."

The third voice that of the leader cut in "Don't be so loud. We're exposed out here. These tracks look very fresh. Sometimes what ever goes in only goes a short distance. Lets tie our staffs together and probe the darkness from here."

Timmy could hear the group busy themselves and he crept closer to the tree trunk that he stood by. In a short time he heard something scratching along the ground. Then, he heard it strike the tree and the group shouted, "There is something in there."

The leader spoke up, "Blog, we'll tie our ropes together and around your waist and you can enter and do a search while we hold on to you."

A spat of cursing followed this. It was obvious that Blog did not relish the thought of entering the dark to look for something that he did not know or that he wouldn't be able to see. He insisted many times that Vinky should do it, only to be told finally that if he did not shut up that they would leave him in the dark. Timmy realized that his hiding place was no longer of any use so he went further into the dark. Suddenly he realized that he had not been able to keep track of the direction he had traveled and that he did not know which way to go in order to leave. He heard Blog stumbling around and suddenly heard a round of curses as Blog ran into the tree. The others laughed with derision and catcalled Blog. "Boy, are you an idiot," Vinky said, "you knew that here was something there and then you stumble into it." Timmy could hear something swish by him and then he felt something just tick him. He realized that Blog must be probing with the staff and he retreated further. Blog shouted, "There is something in here."

"Oh really," came a laugh from the leader, "That would be surprising after all the noise you have made."

Timmy suddenly found that a rock face hidden in the darkness blocked his retreat. To make matters worse he had moved into a crevice and the only way out would be to try to sneak past the searcher. He inched his way ahead hoping not to alert the noisy Blog. Blog suddenly spoke up.

"I'm going to move to where I thought the staff made a small contact."

"Why not tell everyone including whoever is in there what you are planning to do."

Timmy held his breath because he knew that there was no way for him to escape now. Very soon he would be discovered and, if his pursuer was as rough and strong as he sounded, he should fear for his safety. Timmy put his hand to his throat and felt the little pouch that was hanging there. Not having any other course of action in mind he opened the pouch and took the bracelet from its resting place. He carefully felt around until he could place it on his left wrist. He was surprised that the mere touch did not affect him the way it had earlier. He slid his wrist into the band as he heard Blog's heavy breathing getting very close.

Suddenly, Blog let out a terrifying scream and a long litany of curses. "There is something in here and I have never seen anything like this. There was just a bright flash in front of me. Then, a greenish light has started to glow. Get me out of here! I will not stay here any longer."

There was a loud sound of thrashing about and then a thump, followed by a cry of pain.

The group in the light began to ask questions.

"What happened? What's going on?"

"Are you all right?"

"Get me out!" roared Blog and then he let out another string of curses. "Easy, you fools, my foot is bleeding or something. I stepped on something very sharp"

Timmy was very surprised to find, that now that he had put on the bracelet, that he could see in this murk. At first, it was just shadows but then forms began to take shape and become more distinctive. He could see Blog struggling ahead of him and then realized that Blog was no taller than himself, although he was a lot heavier set. He was wearing some type of helmet with a pointed top. He was looking around but no longer seemed to be afraid when he looked in Timmy's direction. In fact, he never made any reaction. Suddenly Blog disappeared and from the uproar and general list of curses Timmy realized that Blog had stepped back into the light although Timmy could not see the border from where he stood. Timmy looked around and then he saw a path of blood that Blog had made. He retraced the path and found his dagger jammed in a crevice. It must have fallen out while he had been trying to get out of Blog's reach. Timmy worked it free from its resting spot and began to make his way back to the edge of the darkness. Blog was muttering and sputtering as the others tied his wound shut.

The leader was saying, "We'll have to hurry back as quickly as we can. Whatever is in there has to be reported as quickly as possible. Do not worry, we won't leave you. The cold water will help by numbing the pain."

"I'll bleed to death."

"Well, do you want to stay here and take your chances?"

"No, no, no!" Blog bellowed. "Idiots, just get me back. Let's get going."

Timmy heard the trio began to move away and he decided that for the time being it was best that he stay within the darkness. He would follow a little later but at a discreet distance.

-15-

Timmy heard the group as they entered the brook and heard Blog's loud complaining as the water flowed over his bleeding wound. Then he saw the trio ahead of him as they entered the realm of darkness. He, however, saw that he was unable to follow the group directly because fallen trees and boulders blocked the way. He was pleased that he was able to see or he could have suffered great injury trying to cross that mess. He surveyed the tangle and decided it was best to detour around it by leaving the darkness for a short distance. As he stepped into the light, he was surprised that it was not bright at all but rather a dull gray. He made a quick scan and moved on to the brook and plunged into the murk once again. He could no longer see the group but could at times hear them splashing along or Blog's cries of pain. He moved forward slowly realizing that the group knew where to walk while he had to figure it out. He knew that the others were getting farther ahead but he did not wish to make a mistake. The water ran by without him even feeling it. When he looked into the water he saw no reflection or evidence that he was even there. He continued to plod on and after rounding a particularly sharp bend was surprised to see something floating in the water. He moved closer and realized that it was a body.

Timmy turned the body over and saw that it was Blog. Was he dead? He could not tell for certain but decided to pull the body to shore to find out. The rest of the group had obviously abandoned their mate when he could not go on. Perhaps, Blog had fainted and they had taken him for dead. 'Not a very friendly group who would simply dump you in the water and leave you to drown,' he thought. Timmy pulled the seemingly lifeless body onto the shore at which time he heard a moan escape from Blog's lips. 'So you aren't dead.' he thought as he took a quick look at the wound. It had stopped bleeding but from the very pale condition of Blog's skin Timmy could tell he had lost a great deal of blood.

Timmy decided that Blog would be all right for the time being. He would have to hurry if he was to catch up to the other two. He decided that he could not worry about traps or holes. He would have to run. After a short time he slowed to catch his breath. He listened but still did not hear any sound. He plodded along for a few minutes then put on another burst of speed. Running in water is not easy usually but somehow it did not bother Timmy. It was as though he was running on a hard packed road. Again he slowed for a rest and he could hear the others. He halted realizing that they too had stopped.

"Did you hear something?"

The leader replied, "I'm not sure, but then what could be out here?"

"Maybe its Blog."

"It can't be Blog. He's dead back there."

"We can't be sure of that. We should have waited to be certain," whined Vinky.

"What and get caught by whatever is out there!! Besides by now the slob will have drowned. What an idiot! Why wasn't he a bit more careful in the dark. He should have avoided that knife. Let's get going"

Timmy heard them moving again and settled into a pace that kept them just ahead of him. After he rounded the next bend they came into view and so he was able to keep them under observation. He saw them reach the line of boulders in the brook and then climb over them to hurry off up the slope.

When he arrived at the spot where he had seen them leave the brook he saw that the pathway up the slope had several lanterns hanging on a rope so that it would be lit up. He did not need the light. He walked up the path and turned at the bend near the top of the slope. There rising up before him was a castle wall. He had not seen the direction the two had taken and though several doorways were visible, he did not know which the two would have used to gain entry. Besides, massive doors barred each entrance. He wandered about checking out the castle from the outside. It was very apparent that there was no way for him to enter that place. He did notice that the castle only had three walls because it was built into a rock cliff, which served as the fourth side. He thought about the castle a bit more and then decided that he had to get back. Suzy would be waiting and if the search party reported its story a larger group might come looking for him. He had no way of knowing whether his disappearing act would hide him from everyone. He slipped back into the water and returned the way he had come. 'So this is the way they make their way through the dark. They can't see so they follow the brook. No wonder they tied a rope on to Blog when he went into the dark. You could get hopelessly lost if you didn't know which way to go.'

Timmy found Blog as he had left him. He was breathing very shallowly and Timmy knew it was only a matter of time before Blog would die. He had lost too much blood. Timmy felt sorry for the fool because it had been his knife that had done the damage.

He knew what he had to do. He reached down and tried to put his hands over the wound. He realized that he could not see where to put his hands because they were not visible. He closed his eyes and thought a moment. He would have to remove the bracelet to make this work. When he would do this it would be completely dark so he had better know exactly where Blog was. More than that he had to know exactly where the wound was. He hesitated and wondered what would happen when he took off the bracelet. He remembered very well what had happened the last time. But he could not wait. Time was running out for Blog and maybe for him. It had to be right now.

Timmy removed the bracelet and immediately he found himself in total darkness. He felt it close in on him and had to fight off the desire to put the band back on. He secured the bracelet in the pouch and then felt his way to the wound. He put both hands over the gash and held it very tightly. He could feel warmth returning to the leg and he could hear a change in the slow shallow breathing of this common foot soldier. 'You are not going to die because of my knife, not if I can help it,' he thought. He allowed his thoughts to go back to the letter that Sapphira had written. She certainly had been right about everything being invisible in the darkness. He wished she had been able to be here right now. Maybe they would have been able to enter the castle to rescue Marlen. 'Now what would happen?' he wondered.

Blog's breathing had become regular and he had stirred a couple of times. Suddenly, Timmy felt him start and sit up quickly with a howl. "What has a hold of me?" he screamed as he jumped up and fell into the water. He cursed and began to splash about. Soon, he was making his way up the stream, hollering and cursing as he went. Timmy waited for him to be clear before he retrieved the bracelet and put it back on. He could well imagine the story Blog would have when he got back. 'I wouldn't want to be those other two. He'll wring their necks for leaving him to be seized by the monster in the dark. He probably won't even think about that wound.' Timmy chuckled as he thought about it. He was relieved that he had been able to help the fool.

Timmy continued to follow the waterway since it was the only way that he knew would take him out of there. He would stop every once in a while to listen for a pursuit but he never heard a thing. Suddenly he stepped out from the veil into the world of light. He was again amazed that it was not bright at all. He wondered if somehow the bracelet did this. 'Oh, yes the bracelet,' he thought, 'I guess I can take it off. No, I'll wait until I'm a bit closer to the cave. That way I should remain undetected. He passed through the narrow crevice and along the path he had followed earlier. He found his turnoff and scrambled over the rocks. He knew that the cave was just ahead over the edge. After all, he had climbed that slope to reach this point.

Timmy carefully reached for his left hand and though he could not see it he could feel where it was. He slowly removed the bracelet. The light burst in on him in a brilliant flash. His eyes hurt and he felt himself becoming very disoriented and woozy. He sought out the pouch by his neck so as to deposit the band. As he did that he felt his knees buckle. The sky began to go around and around, spinning ever faster. Then he knew no more.

-16-

Suzy stirred in her warm blanket and slowly opened her eyes. Suddenly, she realized that she was not in her bed in the little bedroom upstairs in the house she shared with her parents. She looked up at the ceiling at the many painted figures and then it came back to her; this was the cave that the trio had found and used to get out of the rain. She lay there remembering what Sapphira had said about the capture of Marlen and his imprisonment in a castle that was placed in a zone of darkness. She also remembered with a bit of concern that Sapphira had said that Timmy and her were probably in charge of the freeing of Marlen. She had no idea what that really meant but somehow it seemed as though Sapphira was saying that she would not have anything to do with it.

Suzy looked at the paintings again and they seemed to be moving. She realized the movement was likely caused by the flickering of the flames. Still, it left a most interesting impression and effect. She looked a little harder at the paintings and she could make out forest animals that seemed to scamper to and fro. The figures seemed to move through a forest and out into a meadow. There she saw a very strange sight. In the midst of this beautiful painting of a lush flourishing scene was an abrupt end for a black curtain seemed to have been drawn across the rest of the landscape. She looked carefully and it seemed that there were streams flowing out from behind the curtain but she could see nothing within the curtain. She retraced her steps through the scenery and saw that there was a rock face with a crevice within which she thought she could see a cave entrance. She sat up at this sight and, suddenly, she became aware of the fact that she was alone in the cave.

She could see that Timmy's bedroll lay open and that Sapphira's bedroll was no where to be seen. She quickly rose and looked about the cave. She spotted her dried clothing and noticed that Timmy's were missing. She then saw a sheet of paper near her clothing. She left her sleeping area and retrieved the note. It was too dark to read it so she picked up her clothing and moved nearer to the entrance where the light from outside poured in. She put down the paper so that she could change from her sleeping garb into her traveling clothing. She noticed that everything was so clean and fresh smelling. They were not hard like clothing that had dried after being soaked. 'I wonder how Sapphira did that,' she thought, 'she seems like such a great person.'

After changing her clothing, she carefully folded up her sleeping apparel and went back into the cave to put them away in the traveling bag with the many pouches. She then returned to the cave entrance and picked up the note to read it.

> Dear children, I had to leave at once and could not bring myself to waken you from such a deep sleep. Besides, it would have just delayed my parting. I have received word that my presence is needed at once back at the Council and I must use all my powers to return as quickly as possible. I know that you might

be apprehensive about what lies ahead, but rely on your strength, your training and each other and you will be successful. Remember, that in the darkness everything is invisible and that the way to overcome the darkness is to bring forth the light. Until we meet again, I am your friend and servant, Sapphira.

Suzy read the note several times wondering what Sapphira meant by overcoming the darkness. She knew that she had to rely on her strength and all her training. She had already experienced that on the two earlier trips to Gorn. However, she now became concerned about Timmy. She turned over the note and she became aware that there was some writing on the back of the note. It was not very clear and was smudged. She moved closer to the cave entrance and read the faint sketching.

Suzy. When I got up Sapphira had left. I decided to go out and check on this darkness. I won't be gone long. Be careful and check out the cave a bit more in case we have to hide or something. Timmy.

'Oh! It's just like you to sneak off...' she started to think to herself and then she stopped as she remembered that she had been sound asleep. She took the note and returned to the fireside where she added another wood block. She found some food in her traveling bag and then had the remainder of the tea that Sapphira had prepared before leaving on her mission to report what they had seen. She thought about the situation that she found herself in and then made up her mind to begin preparing for the task that lay ahead. She began to explore the inside of the cave and as the sun got higher in the sky she could see deeper into the back of the cave. She could see that this was not a shallow cave but that it really stretched far back into the rockface. She carefully made her way farther into the reaches of the cavern and still the cave went on. She decided that she would keep going until she could no longer see the light coming in the entrance. She noticed that the cave paintings continued, even at this great distance from the entrance. She did not pay much attention to the paintings because she wanted to see how far back the cave went. Suddenly, she realized that the cave took a sharp turn and that she no longer would be able to see the entrance. She also noticed that at that point the walls were no longer covered with any paintings but instead were very dark and almost forbidding. She decided that this was as far as she wanted to go and so she retraced her steps.

Back at the campsite she sat down and thought about what her next move should be. She decided to go out and try to find Timmy. She left the cave and climbed the rocks to a point above the cave that provided an excellent view of the countryside. She looked out in the direction from where they had come and could see that the rolling hills now shone in bright sunlight. Previously as they had passed through those hills, the mist had hid them from view. She then turned her attention to the other direction and spotted what appeared to be a path leading over the rocks. She followed this carefully and soon saw that it led through the rocks and ended by passing between two high towering rocks. She approached the rocks very carefully and hugging the side of the rock in the shadows she peered out across the meadow.

She squeezed back against the rock when she spied movement. She could see two short men in battle clothing down by what appeared to be a black curtain. She was astonished at the immensity of it because it spread out in either direction from left to right without end and rose upward forever. Then a thought came to her. It was the same as the black drape she had earlier observed in the painting in the cavern.

This all was very fascinating. Still she had to be very careful so as to remain unseen by the men down in the meadow. These men appeared to have a rope that went into the darkness like a fishing line that disappears into a lake. 'What could they be doing?' she wondered and then her thoughts were disturbed by shouting. She could hear the men asking some questions and then they appeared to be reeling in their rope, like a fisherman reels in his line. Suddenly another man popped into view and he seemed to be in a lot of pain and consternation. The others quickly wrapped his leg and then the three of them left the rope and disappeared into the darkness in the midst of a brook. She decided to go back the way she had come to check out the entrance to the cave. After she had done that she made her way back to the spot she had viewed the earlier spectacle. She never saw any movement so she decided to go down to where they had been working. The rope lay where it had been left and she could see a great deal of blood had been lost in this place. She felt sorry for the poor man who must be really suffering. She walked up to the darkness and put her hand forward. It disappeared into the murk. She withdrew it and then stuck her head into the darkness, only to pull it back right away. She was very certain that she did not like the absolute blackness that she had just experienced. She decided to pick up the rope and return to the cave. She no longer felt much at ease in this place. Maybe, Timmy would have returned.

She was mildly disappointed on her return to see that her companion had not yet returned. However, she decided that this was probably a good time to go out and find some more wood for their fire. The rain was no longer a problem and the sun would likely have helped dry some of the wood. She made several trips out to do this chore, carefully stacking these logs near the campfire. She decided to make some tea because she had noticed that Sapphira had left the small bag that contained the ingredients for that beverage. She went out to the rock basin and filled the kettle. She decided to take one more look from the top of the rocks. She set the kettle down and clambered to the top. She was surprised to find a still, unmoving Timmy lying on the rock face.

-17-

Suzy stood there looking at the unconscious form of Timmy and immediately she could tell that this was another post-bracelet occurrence. She leaned down and listened carefully to his breathing and noted that it was regular. She knew that she was not strong enough to carry him down to the cave. At the same time, she knew it was not a good idea to leave him in the open. Here, the two of them were likely to be spotted by anyone passing by; so far they had not seen anyone friendly. She reached down and lifted Timmy slightly by placing her hand under his neck. She was surprised to see him open his eyes and begin to get up on his feet.

"Well, you had to try out the bracelet again, didn't you?"

Timmy began to climb down the rock face towards the cave without commenting. Suzy followed and continued to talk. "I saw some strange looking soldier types by the dark wall. Where did you go?"

Suzy waited for a reply and when none was forthcoming, she felt a bit strange. She asked, "Aren't you going to answer?" Still she received no reply. "Turn around and talk to me," she demanded. Timmy continued to climb down the rock face.

When they reached the level area near the cave Suzy grabbed

Timmy's arm and turned him towards her. There was no expression on his face and his eyes simply stared into the distance. Suzy waved her hand in front of his eyes and he did not blink. He turned, walked into the cave and made his way towards his sleeping roll. Suzy followed right behind him ready to reach out to take hold of him if he needed it. He lowered himself to the roll, laid back closing his eyes and his breathing took on the rhythm of sleep.

Suzy found all of this very confusing; yet, she was pleased that they were now in the cave away from prying eyes. She hoped that this cave was not well known to the locals. She found some more wood and placed it on the dying embers. Though it was nearing midday the cave remained quite cool. It was a dry coolness and so did not stick to her; furthermore, the heat from the fire was enough to take away any chills. She returned to where Timmy lay, curled up on his blanket. She reached down and covered him. He did not stir. She decided to take a cracker and have some tea. It was then she remembered she had left the kettle filled with water out by the basin when she had discovered Timmy. She went back to the cave entrance and looked out. Everything was still and quiet. She left the cave and retrieved the kettle. She returned to the cave entrance but she had the feeling that something was out there. She set the kettle down and went back a few steps to the beginning of the crevice in which the cave was found. She could see a group of soldiers like the two she had seen earlier running in the opposite direction along the path that they had followed on their way to this place. She did not venture from the darkness in which she stood because other eyes might be about. She crept back to the cave, picked up her kettle and entered the cave. Then she turned around again to check to see if she had been followed. She also made a careful check that she had not left any tracks that could be followed.

Satisfied that the cave was safe she returned to the fire and placed the kettle on to boil. She knew that from now on it would be very important that the fire be kept from smoking by using only the driest logs and by keeping it rather low. Soon the tea was ready and she poured herself a cup and then sat down on her bedroll to drink her tea and eat her lunch. Having consumed that light lunch, she felt like lying down for a rest. She lay there, staring upward at the scenes that had been painted on the ceiling.

Once again the figures seemed to move before her eyes. She watched, as a story seemed to unfold before her. She watched as a group of rabbits clustered in the meadow dancing and eating and having fun. Suddenly, from the dark curtain by a stream a group of foxes came charging out into the light to surround the frolicking bunnies. The rabbits fought desperately but they were overcome by the superior strength of the attacking forces. Some of the rabbits were slain while the rest were tied together so they could not escape. The foxes then had a feast on the rabbits that had fallen while the captured group had to witness the end of their companions. The foxes then made certain that the remaining rabbits knew what their fate was to be by eating two more of their number. The foxes then took the remaining rabbits and dragged them into the darkness. The rabbits fought but it was in vain. Soon, they had disappeared.

The scene repeated itself but this time the meadow was filled with deer that had come down to graze. The same fate awaited them as their gentler kin before them but, this time the foe was a fold of wolves. Again the captured group was taken into captivity behind the wall of black. The story repeated itself with mice and cats, ponies and cougars, and partridges and hawks. Suzy watched with deep consternation as the gentler group was hustled off as food for the stronger foe. She tired of the scene and moved her eyes back to the cave. Suddenly, she saw a bunny like the one that had been captured earlier dash out of the cave and disappear into the woods. She almost cheered when a deer bounded into view from the cave followed by other creatures. She smiled to herself with satisfaction at the idea that was beginning to form in her mind.

A blast from a hunting horn sounded in the distance brought her to attention and refocused her thoughts on the immediate situation. She knew that there was a search party out there and that it might be possible for that party to stumble into this cave. She knew then that she and Timmy would be like those captured peaceful beasts that never had a chance. She shuddered hoping that those mean looking soldiers preferred normal food. She knew that the two of them could not fight off a hunting group like she had seen earlier. Besides, Timmy was still asleep and would be of little use in a fight.

Another horn blast brought Suzy to her feet. She knew that going out was dangerous but she also knew that sitting here in the cave was like waiting for something to happen. She preferred to meet danger head on. She sneaked back out to the end of the crevice and looked out over the plain. A much larger group had gathered there and seemed to be waiting. The soldiers were drawn up in definite lines and seemed to be at attention. Another group appeared from the woods off in the distance and it fell into formation, as did a smaller battalion that came down the path that they had traveled on. The same thing repeated itself several times as groups showed up from a distance and joined the army that had swollen in size. Every time a new group fell into place, a horn was blasted. Then she noticed a group approaching the assembled army along the path that came from the curtain. The new group stopped and waited for a group from the army to approach it. Suzy realized that these must be the officers having a conference about what was to happen next. The group from the curtain turned and began to march back. The other group fell into place behind and the horn sounded once again. The entire army began to march forward and to reform into four lines marching abreast. It followed the leaders and marched up the road that led to the meadow. Suzy wanted to climb the rock face and go down the path to see where the army was going but she knew that she could then be easily seen. She decided to retreat into the cave and see how Timmy was doing.

As she approached the sleeping figure she noticed that he had turned over which meant that he had started to come out of the deep trance into which he had slipped. At her approach he opened his eyes to see who was coming. Suzy smiled and spoke rapidly, "Boy! It's good to see you stirring. You gave me quite a scare there. You should see all that is going on…"

Timmy shook his head, trying to make some sense of all that had happened. Here he was in the cave in his bed. Had it all been a dream? Had all that he had experienced been nothing but the imaginings of his mind during sleep? He sat up and saw that Sapphira was not here. He saw her note lying on the ground and he picked it up. Then he saw his script on the back of the paper. He reached into his inside pocket and withdrew his knife. It still had dried bloodstains on it. He knew he had not been dreaming, but still something was missing.

"How did I get here?" he asked.

"With all that is happening, all you can ask is how you got here? There is an army outside on the march into the black curtain."

Timmy stared at Suzy. "You know about the black veil that seems to hang from out of nowhere?"

"Of course. Come quickly and very quietly. I want you to see this army that is marching by."

The two of them made their way back through the crevice and Suzy allowed Timmy to stand in front. He stood in awe as the large assembled force rearranged itself into columns and marched away towards the darkness. After a few moments he turned and signaled to Suzy that they should return to the cave. Once inside, they felt free again to resume a conversation.

Timmy began, "Something big is about to happen. First, Sapphira is called away rather suddenly and mysteriously, and then I encountered a group coming out of the darkness. I am sure they were sent to clear the way for this army. However, they came across my tracks instead. If poor Blog…oh that's the name of one of the soldiers who stepped on my knife as he stumbled around in the dark."

"Were there three of them?" Suzy asked incredulously.

"Yes…. How do you know?" Timmy asked.

The two of them sat down and related to each other the happenings of the morning so that each knew what the other had experienced. Suzy was amazed at the story of the castle in the darkness and Timmy was delighted to find out how he had made his way back to the cave.

Timmy took hold of the pouch around his neck and wondered, "It seems that this bracelet makes it possible to see in the dark but tends to blur the daylight. Moreover, it causes one to faint if removed in the light, like the two times that have happened to me. But when I took it off in the darkness I felt no effects. However, it must cause me to glow rather brightly in the darkness at first because poor old Blog really got frightened when I put it on."

"I'm glad you helped him even if he was a very awful man. I hope we don't have to run into him again."

Timmy shook his head. "I was hoping that we could get into that castle but now with all of these soldiers arriving it will be impossible to get near that place. It will be much too dangerous to even try to go back."

"You are not going back that way!" exclaimed Suzy.

"I know, but right now I have no idea what we should so next."

"Well, I know one thing that you really need. You have not had anything to eat for some time. Why don't you just relax and I will get some lunch together. I think the water is still hot enough for some tea."

Suzy busied herself with the preparations for a meal as Timmy leaned back to have a thoughtful rest.

-18-

Emeralda had flown a great distance and she knew that just over the next rise was the entrance to the valley wherein the lodestone was maintained. She also knew that she had to enter on foot due to the many spells that secured the location. She had dropped to the ground near a large oak tree. She had changed her form and had been ready to set out when she noticed a bright shimmering under the tree. She instantly knew what was about to happen. She was now filled with a strange combination of addictive longing and yearning, and a deep dread and loathing for this interruption in her well laid plans. She would have to be quick witted and cunning to turn this misfortune to her advantage.

A bright gleaming figure materialized before her eyes and she bowed her head in recognition of a more powerful being than herself. She murmured, "My lord and king, Chrane, how great thou art!"

The gleaming being strode towards her with a grim smile on his face. "So here you are, my dear friend," he said with a smirk and with extra emphasis on the final word. "You are such a difficult subject to keep track of, always flitting off on some unknown task. If I did not know you better I could almost believe that you are trying to avoid me. But, of course, that can not be, since you chose to cross the borders and have placed yourself completely in my service."

Emeralda again bowed. "You know I am your most loyal subject, dear lord. I regret any upset I may have caused the brightest light in the entire world. I can only assure you that all I have been about is to bring about the ultimate kingdom of our dearest Dark Lord, who has chosen you to be his most wonderful and powerful lieutenant."

Chrane smiled. He enjoyed the flattery directed his way, especially since it came from this fallen Sage. "Yes, yes, Emeralda. You are such a sweet talker, but there is a deep cunning behind all that you do. Still, you have been such a useful ally and servant. You know I give a lot of room, much more than any of the other loyal subjects."

Emeralda smiled coyly, "Oh! I know, dear lord, and I assure you that I am most grateful and honoured. I have just come from the environs of the Sage castle. Few Sages are there. Most seem to have moved to the east towards the great darkness that you have placed over the land. Why they would go there, I surely do not know, since they can't penetrate that veil."

"So that's where you were. I am pleased that you checked out the workings of the council. Fools! Who do they think they are? They can not break through the great wall of darkness, which, my dear, I did not create. It was placed over the land by our most illustrious prince of darkness." Chrane laughed as he took Emeralda's hands and led her in a dance through a large circle.

Chrane stopped the dance and let out a shout. "Now is the time we have been working towards. Soon we will be charge of the lodestone and no one can stop us."

"You are most correct, dear friend and lord. No one can stop us. Once we get our hands on that stone it will be all ours and only ours. Its power will be ours to direct any way we choose. No one else will ever be able to order us to do anything," Emeralda smiled as she winked to her friend.

Chrane paused for a moment. He looked at Emeralda cautiously as the meaning of her words became apparent. He placed his fingers to his mouth as he whispered, "You surely do not intend to challenge our dear lord and master, do you?"

"What has he done for us? We put ourselves in all kinds of danger and what do we get for it? He has taken to following me and harassing me, urging me to become his mistress, and threatening me when I show reluctance. Do I need that? Surely, you do not wish to be a lieutenant forever!" Emeralda said in a mocking tone with special emphasis on lieutenant and forever. "Now is the time for us to make a place for ourselves and the stone offers the opportunity to establish a power base that will overthrow the Sages and will rival that of the dark lord, nay, even be superior to it. You, dear friend, can be a king and I can be your queen." She licked her lips, smiling seductively.

Chrane looked around and assured himself that their conversation was private. His eyes gleamed with anticipation and longing. "We can do it, together, dearest Emeralda. However, how can we get our hands on the lodestone?" Chrane asked.

"I know where it is. I wish I had a princess to carry it to us, but I have been unable to locate a willing servant. So, instead, we will devise a tool to take it. Both of us know that you can't handle it. Moreover, I was seriously injured by my earlier attempt to take it but I will recover from the after effects. One day I will be able to hold it close as my baby. Until then, we need to build a set of tongs strong enough to lift the stone while you block the spell imposed by the Sages," Emeralda explained.

"Of course," Chrane laughed, "that will work. We scurry off after gaining possession of it and find a suitable location to hide the stone."

Emeralda beamed, "I have just the place to locate my baby. It will return to my palace where I will have control over the greatest force that the Sages have created. We will throw up a web of spells and force fields that no one will be able to penetrate. I will be the queen of all," she declared, but then she added quietly, "with you as my king, of course, my lord and friend."

"You know it, my lovely," Chrane laughed evilly, "let's get started. You have a plan already worked out so let's get on with it. What must we do first?"

"Follow me. I have a clearing just over this rise where we can work on the device we will need. Quickly, let's not waste any more time," Emeralda gushed.

The two conspirators hurried down the path and over the rise to begin their project.

-19-

Suzy gathered together some of the cracker-bread and then found some of the dried meat and fruit that had been their staple fare for the past few days. She stared at it and then realized that she too was getting hungry. She was surprised that the sight of this food did not make her ill. Her mother always tried to vary the diet so that one item did not appear too often in a row. However, here she was not the least bit tired of eating the same thing for another time. She checked the tea and saw that it was ready. She turned and began to look at Timmy who had laid back and seemed to be staring intently upward. His eyes seemed to dart back and forth. Suzy turned her face towards the ceiling and she too became enthralled with the figures that seemed to be frozen in a new position, which was different than before. Now the creatures were watching the dark wall because a very bright light seemed to be dispelling it, breaking down its hold over the land and pursuing it into the light. There was no movement but to Suzy the scene seemed to have captured the moment before the wall would finally be torn apart by some tremendous brilliance emanating from within.

Suzy looked at Timmy who became aware of her presence and smiled at her. "Those paintings are amazing, so very lifelike. If you look at them long enough you can imagine movement and the figures seem to begin to relate a story. I was looking at that part over there and it seemed to me a group of wild animals had gathered together and were ripping up a prairie-dog town, forcing those poor gophers to flee. Often they did not escape and ended up as supper for the wild ones. It seemed so very real."

"I know," she said quietly. "Lunch is ready. After we have had something to eat, there is something else I have to add to the story. I did not think of it earlier, but you reminded me of it just a few minutes ago."

The two ate the meal slowly and deliberately, like two gourmets who want to enjoy the taste of a special dish to the very last mouthful. They then sipped the tea and thought about their adventure. Once in a while they would take a look at the ceiling, stare for a moment, and then shrug and return to their tea.

Suzy eventually spoke up. "I mentioned earlier that I did a bit of exploring earlier. This cave goes back a very long way and I never reached the end of it. Almost all the way back there are these pictures, which are so full of life and exuberance. Then suddenly the pictures end and walls are very dark. They don't even seem to cast a shadow or anything."

"It sounds as though the light suddenly ends, doesn't it?" mused Timmy.

Suzy nodded her head in agreement and then she went on to relate the story of the animals that were captured and taken into the darkness. "Somehow these paintings are meant to tell us something. I believe they have messages hidden in them. Some of the animals did escape and they came running out of this cave. Could this cave be the answer to our problems? I had that thought earlier."

151

"By gosh, Suzy, you may have something there. Maybe this cave extends back under the region of darkness. Maybe, that is what the paintings mean. They are the light and they bring the news and brightness into life. The dark area back there may be the beginning of the dark region."

"You mean that this cave might actually extend back into the darkness and have another entrance back there somewhere. Why, of course! That's what the painting is trying to portray when some of the captured creatures come running out of the cave entrance."

Both of the travelers were now getting very excited because they seemed to be coming up with a solution to their problems. Suzy kept on, "Perhaps we can use this cave to actually enter the land of darkness through an unknown gate and somehow spirit Marlen away."

They both paused for a moment at the idea and the thought of the captured Sage. He was the reason for their being on this mission. They knew they had to devise a method to free him. They got up from their meal and headed in the direction of the back of the cave. The light was still very strong so they able to go right to the bend, to the point where the entire appearance of the cave took on a more sinister look. Suzy walked ahead and stopped at the curve. As she peered ahead, she commented, "It's very dark back there." She stepped ahead and disappeared from Timmy's sight. He momentarily felt a surge of panic and felt his hand creep towards the pouch hanging from his neck. Then he saw Suzy's back reappear. She obviously had stepped back, retracing her movement from the dark. "It is very dark past here. Yes, Timmy, I believe you are right. This is the beginning of the dark zone underground."

"But what do we do now? I could use the bracelet to go through the darkness but you would be lost. Besides, I really don't want to use that bracelet again unless I have to. There must be a way, a better way, to use this new entrance," commented Timmy.

Suzy began to look about at the paintings that she saw here. They were frozen in place, unlike those they observed nearer the cave opening. She only looked briefly before she turned away and said, "These are horrid! They are bodies of animals that have been maimed and slashed apart. Does this mean that as we get into this dark area, we will encounter forces of cruelty?"

"Well, some of the pictures that we saw earlier were very unpleasant, weren't they? I do believe that the forces that are holding Marlen are very evil and quite capable of some very horrible actions. We will need to be very careful."

"Timmy, I don't think there is anything else we can discover right here. I think we will have to go back and come up with some idea. Perhaps, we should also go out and check around to see if the army has already gone by."

Timmy nodded in agreement with Suzy's assessment of the present situation and followed her as she made her way back to the fireside. Along the way she paid closer attention to the many paintings. She noticed that most of them close to the dark space were horrible but as they neared the brightly lit zone that they tended to be still pictures of animals engaged in struggles or fleeing from the enemy or the darkness.

After they had returned to the area by the fire, Timmy said, "Let's go out of the cave to see what is happening outide. They took up their places by the entrance of the crevice and looked out. The last remnants of the army were on the road heading for the dark zone. They watched as the army made its way slowly along the road with soldiers coughing in the clouds of dust that had been churned up by those who had passed there earlier. As the last of the troop made its way up the road, Timmy and Suzy nodded to each other agreeing that they should check out what was happening.

They climbed up the path that they had used earlier and slowly crept along in crouched position so as not to be observed. They found the path that both of them had used before and made their way to the twin pillars beyond which the meadow of darkness stretched out. Here they lay behind the boulders and watched as the army entered the meadow further down and then continued on into the darkness by way of the brook that had been used in previous times. This time, however, they saw that the forces were being directed into the darkness by a group which had lined up in two columns between which the army moved towards the dark wall. This group was directed by one individual who stood in a chariot that was drawn by two jet-black ponies. He never made a sign or issued an order but he seemed to command the entire operation. As the last of the troop neared the wall, he suddenly raised his head and began to look around as though he had been disturbed from his task. His gaze became riveted on the spot where the two lay in observation. They knew that he suspected their presence and they wished they had not been so bold as to come looking. However, they could not help themselves in continuing to watch this special individual. He was taller and slimmer than the rest of the army. His armour was coal-black; yet, it glistened in the light. His appearance was that of a confident commander who knew that his army would always follow him. His eyes burned with a deep fire that struck terror in the minds of those that it watched. Suddenly, he raised his arm and the troops stopped moving. He reached down into the chariot beside himself and brought up a falcon with tied legs. These he unfastened and he raised the bird over his head so it could flap its wings in anticipation of its freedom. Then he released it and pointed towards the twin rocks. It screamed and headed toward the place the young adventurers lay hidden.

Timmy moved his hand upwards towards his neck. He felt the bracelet glowing and warm to his touch even though it was still within the pouch. He wanted to remove it from its resting place but instead decided that was not a wise move with the strange commander so close at hand. He looked up and saw the commander staring right at the place that he was hiding. He saw the falcon careening towards this place. Suddenly, he placed both hands around the pouch and squeezed. The warmth began to subside and, as the falcon neared the place in which they lay, it suddenly rose and screeched and headed off in the direction from which the army had come.

They heard a shrill whistle come from the commander and the falcon turned and began to return to the group. The commander waited and then raised his large bow. He fitted it with an arrow and carefully took aim. The arrow was released and it sped towards its target. The unsuspecting falcon continued true on its course towards the commander only to be met with an arrow meant to rip it apart. The arrow found its mark, the bird squawked, and then plummeted to the ground. The commander no longer seemed to be interested in anything except getting his army safely across to the other side of the darkness. Soon, the army had completely entered the dark and just before the commander entered, he turned and stared at land about him. He turned his chariot and rode off into the darkness.

Timmy and Suzy immediately got up and hurried back along the path, their hearts pounding within their chests. They descended the rock face and were soon safely back within their cave. Now, they felt they could breathe easier as they leaned back against the cool rocks.

-20-

Suzy took several deep breaths and wiped her hand across her forehead. She looked up and straight at Timmy who was leaning against the wall of rock inside the cave.

"Did you see how he looked in our direction? It was as though he knew we were there," exhaled Suzy.

"Did you see how he glowered and then sent the falcon to seek us out? I'm sure he knew that he was being watched but did not know by what," added Timmy. "I'm sure it was this bracelet that drew his attention our way. When I put my hand over it I sensed that both he and the falcon lost contact and became confused."

"Could it be your hands?" suggested Suzy. "You know what Sapphira had to say about them having a great deal of strength in them."

Timmy raised his hands before his eyes and looked at them. "They don't appear any different than they always have but they sure have been doing some strange things."

"Well, they can handle that band which really burned me. It's as though the bracelet has no effect over them. Maybe your hands really do overpower the bracelet so that when that commander looked for its power, some force from your hands blocked his sense of it."

"Suzy, that sounds creepy and gives me the chills. I don't know what's going on but whatever it is operates very differently here than back home. Oh well, we can't waste our time thinking about that right now. We have to get down to our task at once or we will be found."

Suzy looked at the concern that was written over Timmy's face and she knew that this was not an idle fear. He really was worried about their safety and being caught.

"Why do you say that? They can not know that we are here or they would have come looking."

"Think about this. Those three thugs came across my path when they were passing by. They quickly returned into the darkness and I could not catch up to the two of them. Then Blog recovers and discovers something is holding him. He already had been frightened by an unexplained strange light glowing in the darkness. Then he returns from the dead or so the others will think. He has recovered and his wound is on the mend. Won't all that create a great deal of suspicion? Now this commander will report what he felt and the dark force inside will know that there is something out here." Timmy explained as he looked from his hands to the paintings and then back to Suzy.

"I'm sure that commander will be none too pleased that whatever it sensed out here has come so close as to even enter the dark area. His army was unable to intercept the mystery intruder," Suzy added.

Timmy turned and looked towards the cave entrance. "That is exactly what I thought. If they come we will be trapped inside this cave."

"But we can't leave here. Sapphira brought us here to rescue

Marlen and I am positive that this cave will lead us to where he is held," Suzy said firmly.

"I believe you are right, Suzy. However, we have to also be concerned that we do not get captured before we can accomplish the purpose for which we were brought."

Timmy's last comment was interrupted by the blast of a horn like the one that they had heard earlier when the army was assembling on the meadow. They quickly made their way to the cave mouth and looked out. They did not see anything and they cautiously made their way to the end of the crevice to get a better view of what was going on beyond the rocks.

The commander clad in black was clearly seen on the road that the army had used earlier. He was now riding his pony and across his saddle he had slung the carcass of the fallen falcon, the one that he had shot when it failed to accomplish the task that had been assigned to it. All around the commander were foot soldiers that were spreading out searching the ground for something. Suzy and Timmy remained well back in the darkness of the crevice but they could see the progress of the searchers and they knew who they were looking for. As the search party neared the crevice entrance the children retreated into the cave. The soldiers approached the crevice but did not look in. Instead, they signaled to the commander with a wave of their arms and a shout.

"There seems to be a crevice or a cave over here but there is something strange about it. Maybe you should come over here and take a look."

The children could feel their hearts beating rapidly and wished they could be elsewhere. However, they did not wish to make a great deal of noise and they felt that perhaps they would be left alone. They could hear the pony approaching and then they heard the commander dismount. Momentarily, they heard a grunt.

"You are right. There is cave back there but it seems that we can't get to it. I can feel the presence of something in that cave but I am unable to determine what it is. Moreover, there is an enchantment over the entrance of this cavern that will not let us in. Maybe Chrane could get through but that double crossing darkling is off trying to carve an empire of his own with that strange, strange lady." He paused for a few moments and then carried on. "Well, let's leave whatever is in the cave where it is but we will set up a guard so that it can not get away. Maybe some time without food will make it a little easier to capture. Right, little sweetie, inside the cave." The commander roared with laughter and the rest of his men joined him. "Now you are caught in a trap and there is only one way out. You might as well make it easy on yourself by surrendering now while we are still in a good mood. I sense that you can be of some assistance to us, whoever you are." The group again laughed as they remained near the entrance of the crevice.

Suzy and Timmy moved further from the entrance and then went over to where the fire had burned down very low. Timmy picked up some wood and put it on the coals. "There is no sense worrying about the smoke being seen now. They know we are in here so I guess we had better look out for ourselves in here. We can not let our fire go out."

"You're right! They can't come in so let's forget about them for the time being. We have our own task that needs to be taken care of," Suzy replied.

Timmy reached down and picked up the paper with the messages that had been written earlier. He looked briefly at the one he had written and then turned it over to read Sapphira's once again. When he came to the last part he read it out loud.

159

"Remember that in the darkness everything is invisible and that the way to overcome the darkness is to bring forth the light."

He looked at the paper again and then set it down. He murmured once again.

"Remember that in the darkness everything is invisible and that the way to overcome the darkness is to bring forth the light."

He shrugged his shoulders. "I know what the first part means. I found that out when I went into the dark. In there, everything is invisible. Everything that goes in vanishes from sight but is still there. In many ways we are like that right now. We are in the cave and are invisible to those soldiers who are now guarding this cave. They don't have any idea who is in here but they know that we are here. It's the last part that baffles me. I am sure that there is something there but somehow it escapes me."

Suzy looked at the paper and then she said, "Bring forth the light might mean using your bracelet, Timmy. Do you remember that when you used it you glowed and that light could be seen in the darkness? Not only that but you were able to see when you wore the bracelet. Maybe that is what it means?"

"I don't think so," interrupted Timmy. "There is something else. I can sense it. I feel that I should not use this bracelet again right now because it has the potential to harm. Besides, it does not help you. There must be something else that has the power that we need."

Suddenly, Suzy jumped up and down and cried out with joy as she realized an idea that had just come to her. "Oh, yes! That's it! Timmy you just got it!"

Timmy stared at her and put his two fingers to his mouth making a quiet signal. "Not so much noise. They will hear us and know who it is. I really don't know what you are talking about. I haven't come up with anything."

"Yes, you have. Don't you see it! Sapphira said, 'the way to overcome the darkness is to bring forth the light.' We need a different light. I have it right here, Timmy." Suzy clutched her hand around the necklace that she had on her neck. "This is it! Remember when we looked at it before. It was brilliant and produced all that light."

Timmy was on his feet now and nearly dancing with the knowledge that had been just revealed. "Of course, that's the answer. You had to bring the crystals with because they sent us that beautiful melody. They were needed for a reason and this is likely it."

"Let's get started," Suzy said hurriedly but Timmy held up his hand.

"We had better prepare a little. We have no idea how long we will be gone so we should take some of our supplies with us. I will take the quiver of arrows and my knife."

Suzy looked about and said, "A good idea. I will take my roll with some food and also my knife. Of course, I will also have the necklace which I have not taken off and you will also have your bracelet."

"We don't know how deep the cave is, so let's have a quick snack before we go. That way we will not have to stop once we enter the dark zone."

They quickly packed the items they felt would be required on their journey into darkness. They were pleased that they had gathered some water earlier and they made certain they had a good drink before they began their snack. After they had eaten some crackers and dried fruit they made their way into the depths of the cave to the region where the light ended and the darkness took over.

-21-

For a moment, the children looked into the darkness, which seemed to have grown more menacing than it had earlier appeared. They felt the presence of a force trying to discourage them by providing images similar to the paintings, which they had found to be repugnant. They heard, or thought they heard, hideous moaning. They could feel fear beginning its cold ascent from their feet chilling every joint and muscle. Suddenly they felt a wave of peace and tranquility wash over them which lifted them into a state of near euphoria, of high ecstasy and an almost dreamlike happiness. All they wanted to do was to return to the cave entrance to enjoy the many joys of this new and promised kingdom. Pictures floated by their mind's eye of wonderful friends who were always there doing everything they wanted. A beautiful palace made of crystal rose up in front of them and the doors opened. A page, dressed in brilliant white, stepped forward and invited them in. Before they could move, several more pages dressed in sparkling black marched forward bearing gifts of coin, perfume and a bowl of the most incredible smelling incense that they had ever experienced.

The first page told them that these and many other riches were theirs by simply entering the gates of the palace. Once inside the palace they would find the crystal thrones that had been forged for the new rulers of Gorn.

The children were caught in a trance-like state as the many wonders were projected towards them. They had not moved, but the desire to follow the wishes of the entrapped consciousness was most appealing and inviting. A struggle was being waged somewhere deep within the minds of these young people as they were surrounded with the promises that were theirs for the taking. Suzy's hand reached out slowly as she groped to overcome the tremendous persuasion that she knew had to be rejected. Her fingers met the searching fingers of Timmy, who too had reached out. As their fingertips touched, they recalled the words of Sapphira

> I know that you might be apprehensive about what lies ahead, but rely on your strength, your training and each other and you will be successful. Remember, that in the darkness everything is invisible and that the way to overcome the darkness is to bring forth the light.

The moment their fingers made contact a bond of resolve and determination was forged between them to resist all of the false promises that they saw before them. They knew that they were being manipulated because the dark force was afraid of the power they possessed. They recalled that they had been told in their Bible classes that only a fool stores up his riches on earth and that man did not live by bread alone. The illusion that they had seen evaporated and all they saw before them was the dark.

Suzy reached up and unclasped the necklace. She carefully took it in her left hand and then reached over to grab it with her right hand so that only the octagonal jewel was exposed. As her fingers curled around the bulk of the necklace hiding both the spherical and multi-faceted gems the still visible crystal began to glow brightly emitting a steady and powerful yellow light that filled the cavern driving back the darkness. The entire region seemed to be filled with new life. The frozen figures painted on the walls began to move and the creatures that had been slaughtered became whole and bounded about. Timmy and Suzy were amazed at the transformation that was taking place throughout the once lifeless zone at this depth in the cave.

Suzy began to move forward towards the dark and as she did the darkness began to retreat. The light from the spherical gem grew brighter driving the shadows from the once darkened region. The walls were covered with a sickly greenish slime and mold which, when exposed to the brilliance emanating forth from the necklet, began to shrivel and glow. The walls became illuminated with a phosphorescent gleam followed shortly by more scenes of wild creatures bounding about in great joy at being freed from their state of imprisonment.

"The walls are painting themselves!" uttered Suzy with a voice filled with awe.

"The slime and mold somehow are transformed into paint to produce these beautiful masterpieces by the light of your gem," added Timmy, as amazed as Suzy had been. "The other paintings must have been produced by the light from the cave entrance."

"Yes, and did you see what happened when I first exposed the jewel? The dead paintings sprang to life as though they had been so far from the light that they had either not been alive or had succumbed due to the lack of light," postulated Suzy, as she continued to move forward.

The moaning that had been evident earlier had turned into a whimpering sound that seemed to scurry away as they approached. The darkness did not flow back in as they went by but instead the walls continued to glisten with new found life. Any initial fears Suzy and Timmy had about wandering in a darkened tunnel were being quickly dispelled by the presence of the light in the cavern.

As they moved, they noticed side tunnels leading off in the darkness. They could not see very far into those regions but they had gained a great deal of confidence in the past few moments that they no longer worried about those places. Moreover, they did not sense anything within the tunnels. Occasionally they caught the scent of decay from deep within the confines of those tunnels but it wasn't anything that increased their apprehensions.

Once, however, they were washed over by a feeling of elation and wonderment as they moved past an entrance. They had paused only for a moment before moving on, leaving that location either to be explored later or to be remembered when the opportunity arose.

As they continued their trek deeper into the cave the ceiling and the walls continued to be transformed and the dreariness and sinisterness of this grotto disappeared providing a haven of hope and peacefulness. This gave them increased assurance that their mission would end in success. Nevertheless, Timmy kept his hand on his bow in which he had placed an arrow so that he could be ready for an attack the instant it might happen.

After walking for an unknown length of time, they came to an open area that had two openings at the other end. Here the walls had pictures of slain creatures and piles of bones. The walls had blackened torches stuck out from them indicating that this part of the cave had been used recently. A faint after scent of burnt wood still lingered. A closer examination of the two openings showed that they were constructed and not natural. The one to the left revealed a series of rock cut steps leading downward while the right opening showed a series of steps leading upward. The two explorers needed to make a decision.

Suzy looked at Timmy for a moment and, then without saying a word, she chose the opening to the left and began to descend the staircase. Timmy followed without comment. Suzy knew that logic indicated that the way out of an underground cave would be to move up but something was telling her that they should go down. She could not explain why she felt that way; she just did.

They wound their way down and they could hear the sound of water dripping somewhere. The walls were damp and glistened with moisture. They did not glow and did not become transformed which amazed Suzy until she realized that they were in hand-hewn tunnels. Suddenly, the hallway opened into another larger room around which there were several large wooden doors.

Closer examination showed that of the six doors only one was closed. They peered into the area behind the nearest door to find a small cell. Suzy turned to Timmy and whispered, "This seems to be some sort of a prison where people are put away in absolute darkness." She shuddered at the thought of being confined in darkness behind a heavy door deep in the earth.

Timmy picked up on her thought. "Even if you did get out of the cell, where would you go? There isn't any light and many opportunities to become lost. I think that this could be a torture worse than death itself."

"We are looking for Marlen and he is supposed to be locked away. Could this be the place that we are looking for?" whispered Suzy.

Timmy pointed to the massive closed door. "If he is here he will be in that cell over there."

They approached the large wooden door and looked for a handle or a lock. There were neither visible. They could not find a handhold to move the door. Suzy leaned forward and called out.

"Marlen, are you in there?"

A quiet voice came from behind the door. "Is that you, princess? Imagine that! You did come for an adventure with me."

"How can we get you out? There does not appear to be any handles or locks?" Suzy asked.

"This door is closed with a charmed lock that is invisible to anyone in the light," came the voice from beyond the door.

Suzy turned to Timmy and said, "Do you suppose that we should extinguish this light?"

"Well, with it shining we can not see a lock," replied Timmy.

Suzy placed her left hand over the spherical gem that had brought light to them on their journey through the cave. Immediately the room became darkened. Timmy looked at the door and tried to see something that appeared to be a lock. However, everything was absolutely pitch dark. Suzy whispered to her companion. "I hear something moving."

Timmy whispered back. "Do not allow any light into this room under any circumstances until I tell you that it is okay."

Suzy was about to admonish him for giving orders when she heard him explain quietly. "I heard it too but if we shine the gem it will simply leave and hide. I am going to put on the bracelet to be able to see."

Timmy put the arrow that he was holding back into the quiver and then reached into the little pouch that was slung against his neck. He felt the coolness of the metallic object that lay inside. He carefully moved his left wrist into the circlet and immediately he heard a short gasp from Suzy.

"I can just barely see you and you are fading quickly."

Timmy used this time when he was still partially visible to retrieve the arrow from the quiver and to get the bow ready. From the opening through which they had entered into this room, he could see a brief flicker of light like that of a torch. However, it was still back up the stairs a fair distance. Even though Timmy could tell the light was some distance back he could make out movement on the stairs. As his eyes adjusted he could see two heavily armed men sneaking down the steps. By the readiness of their weapons he knew that neither Suzy nor himself stood much of a chance should a fight ensue. Their only hope against them would be surprise so he lifted the bow and aimed the invisible arrow at the lead soldier's left thigh. He pulled back and sent the arrow towards the target. A piercing cry split the air as the arrow embedded itself in the flesh of the soldier's upper leg. A roar of curses escaped and a mad scrabble followed as the lead soldier began to claw his way back up the stairs, knocking over his companion who was now gripped by panic. "There is something down there that can see in the dark. I am mortally wounded. Get out of my way before I take another one, fool!"

"Don't worry about me, idiot. I'm not staying around. Fend for yourself," shouted the other soldier.

There was a clatter on the stairs as the two began to beat a hasty retreat up the stairs. Farther up there was a short exchange of sharp words as they rejoined their group. This was followed by a diminishing clatter indicating that the panic of the first two had convinced everyone that the best solution was to get as far away as possible.

Timmy turned from the opening and looked around. He could see that Suzy was still holding her necklace tightly in her hands, almost cowering from the sudden racket that had taken place. He noticed something glowing behind her on the door. He looked carefully and noticed a star shaped emblem emblazoned on the barrier. He felt it and discovered that it was indented. A thought began to grow in his mind. He reached for his left hand and removed the bracelet from his arm and held it between his thumb and index finger on his right hand.

"All right, Suzy, you can provide us with some light now. I have removed the bracelet."

Suzy moved her hand and the room immediately filled with light. However, it did not seem to have the brightness as before and so did not hurt their eyes. Timmy felt the door where he had seen the emblem earlier and when he had found it, he moved his bracelet towards it, guiding it carefully until it matched the indentations on the door. With a twist of his wrist he felt something turn and then he heard a distinctive click. The door swung open.

-22-

As soon as the door opened wide enough, Suzy ran in with her hand still clenching the necklace. Timmy stood by the cell's entrance guarding against the appearance of sudden intruders who might trap the rescuers with the captives. Suzy charged into the middle of the cell and threw her hands around the now standing Marlen.

"How have you been? I have been so worried about you since Emeralda first told us that you had been captured. And then Sapphira told us you were here and then she acted as our guide and brought us to a cave by the dark curtain where we saw a huge army and…" Suzy stopped when she saw Marlen's hand go up in the air and then she broke into a fit of the giggles.

Marlen chuckled and said, "Slow down, little princess. You have come to my rescue. You won't be leaving so quickly that you have to give me all the news in the first five minutes. Come in and have a seat and rest a while. Ask your companion to come in as well. Those attackers won't come back. They are true cowards and I think that an ambush in the dark was the very last straw for them."

Suzy went to the door and called to Timmy that he should come in and meet the most wonderful Sage that anyone had ever seen. Timmy stepped into the cell with an arrow still in the ready. He looked at the old man and slowly put down the arrow. Then he put it in the quiver and slid the bow in beside the arrows. He gave Marlen a deep bow and said, "I am deeply honoured to meet you, most wonderful Sage. Suzy has told me much of you and I have seen you from a distance. I have longed to have the distinct privilege of meeting you."

Marlen laughed. "You are a true young gentlemen. I do believe that our young friend here has exaggerated my importance. 'Most wonderful Sage' is quite a title to be given. I am not worthy of being considered anything but a friend and a servant. I am most pleased to make your acquaintance, young man without a name."

Suzy turned red. "I am truly sorry for such a dreadful blunder. I sometimes need my head turned on again. Marlen, this is Timmy, a true friend, companion and classmate. He has some very special gifts and he has been of great help in finding you."

"I am very pleased to make your acquaintance, young Mr. Timmy. I must say that the two of you really did not waste any time in discovering a way to this place. I had a brief mindtouch from Sapphira earlier today so I knew that you were in the neighbourhood, but I didn't expect a rescue this quickly. Sapphira did not give me any message of substance because it would have alerted the dark force of your presence. She only made contact after she had started on her way back. I could sense that she was in a hurry to get somewhere and then the link was gone. She risked being captured by trying to contact me. I don't know how she did it since a blocking spell has prevented any earlier attempts."

Suzy glowed with happiness at the praise that Marlen had given them. "Isn't she just wonderful, Marlen? She has such a kind heart and is so patient. Not at all like that sister of hers."

"Oh, so Sapphira told you about that. The two of you must have touched her in a very special way because she hasn't spoken about that since the day that Emeralda turned down the road into darkness. Yes, you must have unique gifts to be able to bring that out. Sometimes I worry that terrible memory is too much for her, but she has always shown such good bounce and recovery," commented Marlen sadly.

Suddenly, Timmy wheeled around and drew his knife at the slight sound of a whimper in the corner. There in the shadow of the great door lay a short soldier whose clothing was in tatters. He cringed in the light and whimpered that his eyes hurt him. He didn't raise his face to the group. Marlen said quietly. "A little before you came the guards brought him and threw him into this cell. They laughed and said I probably needed some companionship. He never said much but from the sound of his breathing I could tell he was hurting. I have tried to settle him down so I could try some healing, but he just continues to moan and refuse any help."

Timmy looked at the figure and then bent over to try to get a better look at the face. There was something about this man that he wanted to ascertain. He moved closer to the cringing figure, which had shrunk back against the wall. Suzy moved up closer so as to provide better light for Timmy.

"I do believe that this is Blog, Suzy! But why is he here and what are all those terrible gashes and half bleeding slashes?" asked Timmy. "I wonder how this could have happened."

Marlen spoke up, "This is what I have been able to gather about this poor fellow. When he was tossed in here, the guards reviled him and kicked him. They said that he should have died and that now he was a true enemy of the commander. They said that he had been lucky to get off with only seventy lashes. They threw him into the corner and he has not moved since. He just whimpers and shrinks away if I try to help him. He keeps moaning about having to go into the dark and seeing strange things with greenish glows. He is afraid of hidden things coming up on him and grabbing him in the dark."

Timmy moved closer towards the half curled body in the corner. Suzy followed closely behind holding up the necklace to flood the area with light. Blog had nowhere to go and began to plead that they leave him alone with all his terrible wounds. Timmy could see that the poor wretch was indeed in great pain and needed help at once. He knelt down before Blog and slowly reached out towards his right arm, which was badly beaten and swollen. "Easy does it, old timer. I want to help you. Please give me a chance to do something about these terrible slashes before you really begin to suffer. I am just going to put my hand on a few of them. Don't be nervous."

Blog shivered and pleaded, "Don't hurt me, young fellow. I am hurting too much already."

"I will not hurt you." Timmy put his hand on Blog's arm and kept it there even though Blog's initial impulse was to jerk his arm away from him. Timmy then brought up his other hand and placed it on the same arm. Blog closed his eyes and began to sigh quietly and began to relax indicating his pain was subsiding. Timmy turned to Marlen and Suzy and indicated that they should sit down. "This will take some time. There is so much damage and healing will be a long process."

Suzy turned to Marlen who had returned to his stool. "We met Sapphira and she is such a delightful person."

"Yes, indeed, she is that. And this friend of yours has some special gifts, I see. A gentlemen, a warrior, a locksmith with a heart of gold and he possesses the gift of healing. I will want to talk more with him later when he has had the chance to complete this task. Come now, I want to hear about your adventure so far. Before you start, perhaps we should have a little lunch, if you were prepared enough to include that in your traveling bag."

Suzy smiled with pleasure at the thought that she would be actually providing something for her wonderful friend. She unrolled the pack and spread it on the floor of the cell. She took out some of the bread, dried meat and fruit and set it in an attractive arrangement. Then, she invited Marlen by gesture to begin. She turned to Timmy, who now had his hands around Blog's other arm. "Do you want a bite to eat, Timmy?" He shook his head before he spoke up. "Perhaps a bit later. I would like to complete the healing process, which is progressing very well. His pain seems to have dropped dramatically."

Suzy turned to face Marlen and she observed that he had already started to eat some of the rations that had been spread out before him. Suzy also took some of the food since she now felt quite hungry. She did not have anything to drink. Marlen brought forth a bucket that was sitting along the wall. He reached in and brought up a metal cup filled with rather brackish appearing water. He had a short drink and passed it to Suzy. She could only manage a short sip. It tasted metallic and bitter. She decided that she could go for a while yet before she would really need a drink.

"It really does not taste too good, does it? I've become quite used to it after being locked in here for all this time. This food tastes like a banquet since I have not been fed for such a long time."

Suzy stopped eating and stared at the old man. "How do you manage to go for such a long time without eating. I would simply starve."

Marlen chuckled. "I have noticed how much food you are able to put away. I believe we could feed an army on the amount you must eat in a week."

Timmy laughed at this point and received a gentle slap on the back of his head from Suzy. "That's enough from you," she said. "No, Marlen, I am not trying to be funny or display my ignorance. I really want to know how you do it."

"Well, Sages have learned that we can sustain life for a long time without eating. Usually we eat to be friendly and that type of nourishment is sufficient to keep us in good health for a very long time. We can go for very long stretches of time without a meal. When we guard the lodestone we do not eat during the entire cycle. We draw our strength from the link we have forged with the rest of the Council of Sages. I cannot really explain how or why we can go for so long without food, but I do know that every Sage has that ability. Anyway, that is enough about me. Tell me about your journey."

Suzy told Marlen about the adventure from when it started with the singing crystals, the step through the triangular hole, the supply shop and the long walk through the never-ending rain. She continued with the cave and the note from Sapphira and then finding Timmy. She told about the cave and then the army that marched by. She did not forget to tell Marlen about the paintings and then the entrapment by the dark commander. She ended her story by relating their descent into this place and the attack by the guards.

Blog opened his eyes as Timmy placed his hands over the last of the terrible lash marks. He looked at Timmy for a very long time and then slowly he said. "You were back there in the dark, weren't you?" Timmy nodded his head as Blog continued. "I was wounded and bleeding badly. I remember the pain getting sharper and stronger as I stumbled along the creek. I tried to call out but the other two just laughed. I remember stumbling and then I was gone. I remember now that when I woke, someone had a hold of me. I recognize the touch. It was you, with your special hands, because my wound then was healed. I ran off and made my way to this castle where I tried to tell my story. But no one would believe me and some even said that it would have been better if I had died. That one in black was the most awful with his deep fiery eyes. He ordered me lashed to get the truth and, when I could not tell him about you because I had not seen you, he threw me down here. Yes, young healer, I know you and I really want to repay you. But I need to know why you would help me, a total stranger and foreigner to you."

Timmy looked at Blog for a moment and then said quietly. "You are a brother to me. We all are and we should come to the rescue and aid of any member of this large and special family." He lifted his hands from Blog who now smiled and rose to his feet

Blog bowed to Tommy and thanked him for such wonderful care, "I am truly in debt to you, young healer. I am very grateful for the care you have provided. Thank you so very much." Timmy led him to where the other two had finished eating and had been listening to their conversation. He invited Blog to sit down and take part in the meal that was spread out on the traveling pack.

-23-

After they had eaten their meal, Blog suddenly stood up and asked, "Why are you helping me? I was going to harm you but now you are treating me so well. What do you want from me?" Blog's face was a mix of confusion and deep consternation.

Suzy said quietly, "You really do not understand. We do not hold feelings of anger towards you. You were wounded and needed help. Timmy, through the use of his special gift, was able to provide some healing for you. He did not expect any repayment from you. Can you understand this?"

Marlen rose and placed his hand on his chin. "No, he can not understand why you would do this. It is not the way that things are done in Gorn. Moreover, Blog has been a slave of an evil taskmaster for so long that he can only expect the very worst from everyone. If someone does anything for him, there must be a hidden motive of gain. I think we in Gorn have a great deal to learn from people from your place."

"Don't get Suzy wrong, Marlen!" interjected Timmy. "There are many people back in our place that also do whatever will get them ahead without any regard for those around them. There are, however, many who believe like us that there is a better way to act towards their fellow man, a way of love and caring."

Blog spoke up, "I do not understand this at all. You come here to rescue this Sage and then you take time to help a wretch like me. I am indebted to you and because you have saved my life, I will now acknowledge you as my master." He bowed before Timmy. "I will follow you and attend to your needs. I will be your servant and should the time come, I will save your life, not once but twice, like you did for me." He bowed again to Timmy.

Timmy was quite taken back by this and did not know how to respond to this sudden development. He looked to Suzy and then to Marlen with eyes filled with pleading. Marlen held his hand up before his mouth asking Timmy to be silent. Marlen stepped forward and took Blog by the arm.

"Stand up, Blog. The young master is not familiar with the ways of which you speak. He must be told that when one saves another's life, the saved one becomes a servant until the debt can be repaid. The young master accepts your wish to follow him and welcomes you as a member of his party until such a time as the debt is over."

Blog rose and Timmy was about to protest but decided that such would only prolong the difficult situation. Besides, Marlen probably knew how to handle a tricky situation like this better that he did.

Marlen turned to Suzy and said quietly, "I think the time has come for us to move on to the next task at hand. We must somehow drive this darkness from the land so that the Dark forces cannot use it as a base of power and as a prison for their enemies. Lead the way, young princess."

Suzy had been gathering up the contents of her traveling bundle and now she asked Timmy to tie it up, since she held the necklace in her hand. Timmy obliged her and placed the bundle on her back. Then, she led the small party from the cell and up the steps. Marlen followed close behind her with Blog next in line. Timmy brought up the rear, having removed the bow from the quiver and cocking it with an arrow. They made their way up the winding stairs and finally reached the room that attached to the cave. They paused there for a moment and Suzy looked at Marlen for a suggestion of what to do next. She did not see any signal in his face or eyes, so she waited for another few seconds to collect her thoughts. Then, she turned and proceeded up the steps into the darkness towards a destination that she had never seen. No one questioned her decision and each fell into his place in the line up. She passed through several small rooms and finally came to a larger room, which had windows that looked out into the darkness of this veiled land.

The group assembled near the windows and looked down on the courtyard of a castle. Another window on the other side of the room in which they were gave them a view of a road leading up from a brook. The road was partly illuminated by a series of lamps along the borders. Timmy looked out for a moment and then spoke up.

"This is the castle that I saw in the darkness. That road comes up from the brook that is used as a guide for travelers wanting to leave this region for the land of the light. It was along that brook I found Blog near death. I used the power of my hands to heal those wounds."

Blog grunted at the reminder of this incident.

Except for the light that the torches cast for the pathway and the courtyard, darkness covered all of the area surrounding the castle. It was as if nighttime had fallen over the land. It created a dreary, gloomy, almost morbid atmosphere that easily affected the inhabitants by spreading depression and despair. There was a sense that this darkness had covered this area for almost too long—that the point in time beyond which recovery would never be truly possible was very near.

The party of light stood by the windows looking out for some time. Suddenly, there was a noise in the courtyard. Someone was shouting and soon a bell was tolling. Many figures ran into the courtyard and began to look up at the tower in which the light party was situated. Timmy looked out the window overlooking the stream and saw a large group of men assembling and pointing upward at the window where he stood.

"It looks as though they know we are here. I wonder what the next step is going to be," queried Timmy.

"I expect that we will be attacked," volunteered Blog. "It is the strategy that this commander usually uses. He never stops to assess a situation; he sends his troopers out to do battle without any thought for the strength of his foe."

"We should be able to hold off an army from here," Marlen observed. "We are high enough up to make most arrows ineffective and the passage way into this room has a long straight portion down which any attackers must travel before reaching us. They can easily be picked off with carefully placed arrows."

"Hopefully not too many make the attempt since my supply of arrows is limited," Timmy added, as he counted the number of missiles in his quiver.

Suzy moved from window to window, noticing the stir and commotion that the light from her crystals was creating. She was fascinated by the growing mob of enemy soldiers who seemed to have turned their collective attention to the light coming from the tower window. She entered a small room at the far side of the first room. She looked about and spotted a closed door at the other side of the room. Suzy walked slowly and deliberately towards it. She listened at the doorway for a moment and then unlatched the massive door and swung it open. Before her was a darkened passage with a steps leading upward. Marlen stepped up behind her.

"Well princess, I believe you have found the stairs to the top of the tower and the turret that overlooks the entire courtyard and castle grounds", he commented.

Before Suzy could respond to this statement, Timmy shouted, "Someone is coming up the stairs. It sounds like a fairly large group of soldiers by the amount of racket they are making. Obviously, this is not meant to be a surprise attack." Suzy turned and went back into the first room, followed by Marlen.

Timmy readied his arrow and then he saw Blog standing to the side. He could see that the new member of this group felt out of place, yet displayed readiness to help if given a chance. Timmy drew out his knife and handed it to Blog.

"Here, Blog, use this if it is necessary."

Blog looked at the knife for a moment and then looked at Timmy. "You trust me enough to give me a weapon. What would happen if I turned on you and stabbed you in the back?"

"What's the difference? We might be overrun by the enemy and all be stabbed. If I trust you, then there are two fighters against their numbers. I feel that makes our chances a little bit better. There is no more time for debating and talking. Just be careful with that knife. You already have been wounded by it."

Blog grunted an acknowledgement at the logic his young master had shown. At that moment, the enemy soldiers burst into the passageway and began running towards the room filled with light, without any regard for an ambush or for their personal safety. Timmy waited a moment and let his first arrow fly. It sped towards its target and buried itself in the upper chest of the lead fighter. As he fell, screaming, to the floor Timmy aimed and fired his second arrow catching an attacker in the upper thigh. A third arrow entered a soldier in the resting area between the shoulder and the chest. The fourth and fifth attackers had come to a stop and had begun to backtrack from that place, unsure of how many archers were firing.

A sharp order to charge came from further back. "Attack, you cowardly fools! Why are you backing up? Do you want your heart served on the plate of the commander, you liver hearted swine?"

The attackers, who had stopped their retreat to assess their situation, yelled and charged ahead again, filled with a resolve that death was better than the fate that waited their failure. Timmy's next arrow struck the lead runner square in the chest and he stumbled headlong forward. Suddenly, the entire party in the passage way came to a halt and let out a mournful groan. Suzy had come across the room and had stood in the doorway behind Timmy. The necklace shone brightly in her hand and its light had begun to throb. The soldiers gazed fearfully on the slender figure of a girl before them and as the light intensified, they began to retreat slowly, some dropping their weapons in the hallway. They let out another collective moan and turned in full retreat. A sharp clatter was heard, over which a voice was barking commands to attack. A spat of curses was followed by a cry of a wounded man and then the noise subsided, as the soldiers fled from the tower.

Suzy walked slowly down the passageway and each of the fallen soldiers tried to shrink away. Blog came up behind her and raised his knife to kill the first soldier lying in the hallway. Suzy turned, looked directly at him and issued an order. "Put away your weapon, Blog. These men need help, not further injury. Put away the knife and then collect the weapons from each of these men so that they will be out of harm's way. Timmy, come out here and see what you can do for these men. Start with the most severely wounded and see if you are able to undo the damage that has happened here." Suzy had taken control of the group and even Marlen had come into the passageway and was helping to make each of the wounded men more comfortable.

Each of the fallen was quaking with fear. They did not understand the powers that had captured them. The light that the princess held seemed to rob them of their ability to act, but it did not dispel the fear that they felt overwhelming them. They did not understand the strange behaviour of their attackers who now seemed prepared to assist them.

Marlen moved beside Timmy and said, "Put your gift to work, young man. If you need assistance I can try some healing as well, but I fear that my strength may not be there for a prolonged session"

Timmy moved among the wounded and placed his hands on their injuries. They were amazed at the rapidity at which the pain ceased and the feeling of relaxation that this young man gave to them. Timmy had gone first to the soldier he had last felled and had quickly removed the arrow from his chest. Though the gaping wound had looked serious he placed two fingers in the hole to stop the bleeding and then placed his other hand over the wound. The bleeding ceased immediately and, as he withdrew his fingers, the wound began to mend itself. Satisfied that the situation had stabilized itself, he moved on to each of the next three soldiers tending to their wounds. As he completed his first round, he noticed Marlen returning from the stairwell with another man whose right arm was almost severed. This took more of his skill but presently the arm began to recover. Marlen had disappeared and when he returned he simply shook his head.

Blog had been busy picking up and storing all the weapons in the room. He shook his head in disbelief. He obviously did not comprehend what was going on. After Timmy had completed a second round of healing, the four adventurers met together to discuss what had happened.

Blog asked abruptly, "Is it wise to help these? What happens if they attack us?"

Timmy turned to him and said a bit sharply, "Blog, you have such a short memory. We did the same for you. Should we have left you? No, of course not! That is not the way this party works."

Suzy turned to Marlen and asked, "What did you mean by the shake of your head earlier when you went into the staircase?"

Marlen said rather solemnly, "There is one out there who is beyond help. His comrades have cut him down. If the enemy force returns, these soldiers will be killed first as traitors. If they try to starve us out we will not have enough food."

Suzy said quietly, "I think the time has come for this horrible darkness to come to an end. I must ask Timmy and Blog to remain here with the soldiers while I go up to the top of the tower. I want you, Marlen, to come with me. I do not believe you will need any light while I am gone," she said to Timmy.

She turned and walked back into the little room. No one protested or questioned what she intended to do. Marlen followed her and they began to ascend the stairs that opened abruptly on a platform with room enough for one person. It was surrounded with a low railing of cut stone. Marlen remained behind on the staircase.

Suzy raised the necklace so that the light spread out across the immediate vicinity. A cry went up from the assembled group in the courtyard as they surged forward waving their swords at her. The sound of arrows striking the walls far below could be heard and then the futile curse of a mass that was powerless. They stood in awe of the small girl that had their rapt attention. Suddenly, the light at the top of the tower was gone.

Suzy had covered the spherical gem and its light had ceased to flow. She waited a moment and then removed the many faceted gem from its place of hiding. It began to pulsate with colours of every hue and shade. The assembled body let out a cry of amazement and, then, began to raise their hands to cover their eyes for the intensity of the illumination was becoming unbearable. The mob moved back and the light grew in brilliance. They felt their flesh begin to warm and their weapons began to glow. They screamed at the heat of these instruments and dropped them to the ground. The massive crowd was in a mad retreat as the light grew brighter and brighter. The darkness over the land rapidly retreated like the army of darkness.

The light of the crystal broke the veil of darkness and a bright harvest moon shone over the landscape revealing many scurrying figures—each trying to hide from the new light that shone over the land. The stars sparkled with newfound brilliance in the sky above. Suzy covered the many faceted jewel and exposed the round one to provide the necessary light with which to descend the stairs with her companion and friend.

-24-

Suzy and Marlen re-entered the passageway where Timmy and Blog were tending to the needs of the wounded soldiers. Suzy indicated that they should go and look out the window. Blog let out a low whistle when he saw the landscape bathed in the soft glow of moonlight. He did not wish to leave the window. He was seeing the starlight over this castle for the very first time. This had been home for him since his youth.

Timmy was pleased at the transformation and took it all in, for a brief moment before returning to his patients. The wounded had become much more at ease with Timmy. They could sense the power that his hands possessed and the caring his heart displayed.

Marlen called Timmy and Suzy for a short meeting. "We can not stay here. I have made a mind link with the Sages who are advancing and they warn that if we stay in this place, we are at great danger. Something is on the move and it threatens the land that once was dark. I did not get a clear picture but it wants to avenge itself on this castle. Whatever it is feels this place is the source of all the trouble that occurred. To travel overland to the former edge of the curtain could be hazardous."

Timmy spoke up, "We could return by way of the cavern through which we came. I know we still have to face the soldiers beyond the entrance but we will be away from this place."

Suzy interrupted excitedly, "Yes, Marlen, please let's go that way. I would really like you to see the living paintings. The way underground would provide a safer path back."

"That is probably the best answer to our present problem. However, we have to think about these soldiers," said Marlen.

"I believe they are fit to travel. Let's see. Men, get up on your feet," ordered Timmy.

The five soldiers stood at attention immediately, a little concerned at the order and a little apprehensive at the changing state of affairs. Timmy approached them and said, "You are free to leave at once. You must leave and try to get away from the castle because some forces are at large that threaten to destroy this place."

The soldiers murmured a bit and then formed a small huddle and talked to each other. After a few words, they turned and faced Timmy. The one who had almost lost an arm stepped forward and said, "We do not wish to go across that evil land again. You have done us a great service when it was your right to have killed us. You made us whole and for that we owe you our allegiance. Where you go, we will follow."

Timmy called Blog forward and then said to the soldiers, "All of you are familiar with Blog, who is my lieutenant. He is now placed in command over you and you will dutifully follow his instructions. He will be your commander."

The troop grinned at the thought of the once simple and foul-mouthed Blog being in charge. They acknowledged their support for the novel idea by raising their hands in a salute. Then, Timmy ordered Blog to march the group into the next room and to equip them with the weapons that had been taken from them. The soldiers looked surprised, but Blog said, "That's the trust that master Timmy puts in all of us. Better get used to it. It will feel a bit strange and unbelievable at first but there it is." Blog marched the troop into the next room while Marlen came over and placed his hand on Timmy's shoulder.

"You, indeed, are a prince, young man. You have a great gift and someday this world will rejoice in all that you have done."

Timmy hung his head as his face turned red at the special praise that this wonderful man had given him. He stammered a very quiet, "It was nothing!"

Suzy spoke up then, "It was not nothing, Timmy! You did a great and noble thing by helping those poor and helpless soldiers who had no mind of their own. They were driven by fear and you have erased it, so that, now, they wish to serve you out of loyalty."

"Suzy is right, young prince. You have done well," added Marlen.

At that moment, Blog led the troop into the hallway and this was the cue for Suzy to take the lead. She moved ahead with the necklace held high to provide light on the way back down the stairs. Marlen fell in behind her followed by Timmy. The group of soldiers brought up the rear and had their weapons ready should they be attacked. They moved down the stairs past the body of their former commander, whose head had been removed during the brief struggle in the stairway. The men looked only momentarily at the gruesome sight and, though they felt some relief that this wicked master was dead, they felt a deeper dread at the thought of what the greater commander, the one in black, would do them if they were ever returned to his ranks. Instead, they looked at the stout back of Blog and the small figure of Timmy and were reassured that they were now safely out of the reach of darkness.

After a descent without incident, they reached the cave entrance and they moved into the cavern. They noticed that the walls no longer had paintings of creatures but they still glowed, giving off a pale yellow illumination that was sufficient by which to see. Suzy finally was able to put down her hand and place the necklace around her neck. They did not stop and, presently, they came to a region in which the walls were covered by paintings. The party stopped because Marlen and the soldiers were amazed at the lifelike quality of these images. Suddenly, one of the soldiers cried out, "They are moving. Look they are running away."

The group realized that the paintings, indeed, were moving away from the castle and were fleeing as fast as they could move. This gave the group added incentive to continue its trek away from that place of danger. They were able to keep pace with the paintings but could not pass them.

Suddenly, they felt the ground shudder beneath their feet and there was a sudden jolt, which caused them to fall to the ground. Pieces of rock debris cascaded down on them but none were of a size to do any damage or injury. All of a sudden, a cloud of dust rolled through the cave from the direction of the castle.

Marlen rose and said, "I believe the cave has now been sealed so that we can not be followed. We have only one direction to go now. It's a good thing we have already chosen this direction."

As the dust cleared, the group became aware of another phenomenon that was different. The paintings were no longer fleeing and were, indeed, moving back into the cave from which they had taken flight. However, their journey back was not that of hurried flight but one of leisurely paced dancing and leaping. The group stood and watched this panorama for a while and, then, moved on towards their destination. All of a sudden, they burst into the area that marked the end of their journey. They moved towards the area of the fireplace that now only contained the white and grey ashes of embers that had long since grown cold.

Timmy and Suzy realized that they had been awake for a very long time, but neither felt very tired. They looked towards the entrance and saw that the sun had begun to shine through, telling them that an entire day had passed.

Suzy moved towards the entrance because she knew the enemy still lurked beyond that opening. This was an enemy still to be overcome or all that had been done to this point would have been in vain. Timmy followed and Marlen fell in behind.

Suzy walked the short distance to the end of the crevice in the rock and stepped into the daylight without stopping to see what was beyond. Obviously, the guard was caught completely by surprise because they did not even notice the three strangers for a few seconds. During that time, Suzy had removed the necklace from its resting place and now she held it high over her head. The guards began to scramble to their feet and one shouted an alarm. Suzy released her hold on the spherical gem from which poured forth a reddish light. The soldiers began to advance towards the trio with weapons drawn amid shouts and rough laughter. The gem began to glow a light purple hue that slowly deepened. The soldiers fell back as though struck by an invisible mallet. As the light intensified, they began a rapid retreat and soon were in full flight from the awesome force of the necklace.

Suzy became aware that there was one figure that was not fleeing. Instead, the commander dressed in black mail was advancing on his mount. He paid no heed to the light that was being emitted from the crystal; his eyes were riveted on the girl. Timmy had readied his bow with an arrow and was prepared to launch an attack at the opportune moment. The black commander fixed his stare on the eyes of the girl and locked her gaze to his. He spoke quietly with a voice that seemed as smooth as silk and as sweet as honey.

"Young miss, you, indeed, are a fantastic foe. You drove away these mere soldiers, but I have no fear of that little bubble in your hand. I do not wish to harm you so I will ask you to please put it down and surrender yourself into my care. We could do so much together. We will set up a kingdom that will rival that of the dark and the light."

As he spoke he kept his gaze firmly fixed on Suzy and she seemed absorbed with his growing presence. His arm dropped slowly to his side and he drew forth a very dark and evil sword. Still, he advanced and then Suzy spoke.

"Advance no farther!"

The dark lord stopped his progress.

"You have come as far as you may without bringing destruction on yourself. Should you fail to surrender now you will be destroyed," Suzy said firmly.

A cold fear flowed through the commander and for a brief moment he lost his eye contact with the girl as he noticed the boy raise the bow into firing position. He knew that he was beaten but the deeper fear of losing overpowered him. He raised the sword and nudged the pony ahead.

Before Timmy could fire, Suzy released her grip over the other two gems; the three began to glow intensely. The entire area was bathed in a pulsating rainbow of hue. The commander's eyes lost their focus and, suddenly, he screamed as the light struck him. He was carried upward and began to roll over and over, becoming a transparent ball of gas. Suddenly, the cloud of gas began to disappear into a spot in its midst. A terrifying scream came out of the gas and, then, as the cloud disappeared there was the sound of armour rattling to the ground. The black mail lay formless on the ground.

Suzy lowered the crystals and looked at them. They no longer glowed but appeared as lifeless as they had while they lay in her dresser drawer. She replaced them around her neck and turned to the other two.

"I'm starved. I wonder if there is any food left in our traveling sacks."

Timmy and Marlen laughed at the heroine. They went back into the cave to discover that the soldiers under Blog's able command had started a fire, set out a meal and boiled some tea. They all laughed together and then sat down for a well-deserved meal. After the meal was eaten, the group entertained themselves with songs, stories and a great deal more laughter. Much later Suzy and Timmy left the group, found their bedrolls and soon were sound asleep.

-25-

The two partners in deceit and conspiracy had fashioned a large set of tongs from a fallen oak. Chrane and Emeralda had moved fluidly, using skills that humans could only envy. Their creation looked like a large two tined fork. Its length was at least three times Emeralda's height. The handle was about the thickness of her head. They stood back and admired their handiwork, but Chrane seemed distant and distracted. Emeralda had paid little attention to her colleague during the manufacture of the tool, but now she became aware that he seemed pre-occupied.

"My lord," she cooed, "do you not appreciate what we have done? We are close to achieving a goal that will change our destinies."

Chrane looked at Emeralda with a combination of fear and disdain. "I sense some great disaster looming. Everything is not aright within the veil of darkness. I think I should have been there. My captain has perceived the presence of an unknown force which has led to a great sense of foreboding."

"But, lord, you can't go now when we are so very close to gaining the stone of power. With it, we will be able to correct any problems that may arise. We just need a bit more time. We stand on the threshold of a future of grandeur," pleaded Emeralda.

Chrane's eyes flickered back and forth indecisively. Then, he grinned, "Of course, my queen. We have come too far down this path to stop now. However, I sense that we must act quickly before circumstances beyond our control wipe away our opportunity and turn triumph into disaster." He laughed hideously.

Emeralda raised her arm and the tong rose into the air. She moved swiftly and the tool glided along as if it were weightless. Chrane strode along side, pleased with the efforts of his aide.

Emeralda and Chrane descended into the valley on foot. Off in the distance on the valley floor a small creek wound its way. A large stone castle stood near the creek. High on one of its towers a flag idly moved. Chrane grinned again.

He said enthusiastically, "So this is where they have hidden it. Cleverly done, because this vale is almost inaccessible and very hard to detect. You are such a loyal friend and ally. Your skills and knowledge add so much to my quest. I want you to know how greatly I appreciate you," Chrane bubbled.

"My duty is my pleasure, lord," Emeralda replied, flattering her partner. She shifted the load so that the tong could pass through a narrow opening in the trees that now lined the pathway on which they were making their way. In a moment, they emerged from the trees on the valley floor to view the castle gates straight ahead of where they were, but still at some distance. Chrane was walking more slowly as he carefully surveyed his surroundings, wary of hidden foes. He was also struggling against the force fields that the Sages had put in place to protect and secure the lodestone. He had to deliberately push himself forward as he felt himself being repulsed. It was like walking into a gale-force wind; it required a great deal of energy to continue to make progress.

The gates opened as they walked up the steps leading to the entrance. Emeralda moved the fork through the doorway and concentrated on her task. She did not notice that Chrane had stopped climbing the stairs. He displayed a deep dismay. He held on to the stone edge of the stairs with such a force that the stone began to crumble. He became very distant. Emeralda sensed that he had stopped walking. She eased her load to the floor and turned to find her partner.

She could tell that something had happened by the look of horror on his face. "What do you see, my lord?" she asked, perplexed that their quest was being interrupted. She knew she had reached farther than was a safe risk and she knew also that their time was very limited. She had counted on events elsewhere keeping all their foes occupied. "Is everything alright?" she asked.

Chrane turned to Emeralda, his eyes filled with dread and deep consternation. He stared at her, obviously trying to re-orient himself to his surroundings. He looked around and then focused on the lady in black. Suddenly he burst out, "Oh my goodness, Emeralda! We have serious problems. I should be back there. The veil has fallen. The darkness is gone. The castle is in ruins. Marlen has been freed. The dark commander has those responsible trapped in a cave, but he can't move against the spells that protect the hiding place. I should be there. What do we do?" Chrane asked, with a voice filled with anguish.

"Those brats! They did get through to rescue him. I wanted to stop them but I couldn't." Emeralda stared at her partner and then looked around, her attention becoming fixed on the fork that lay on the floor. "We must get back to our task at once while we have time. We are standing on the edge of an abyss and its edges are beginning to crumble, threatening to take us to our destruction. Let's get the stone and get out of here as quickly as we can," she said urgently.

She wheeled away without waiting for a reply. She was desperate for she felt all her plans and work were in danger of slipping away. She raised the tong and hurried ahead into the next room from which a blue light was pouring. Chrane followed quickly, knowing he was lost if they did not succeed at once.

On a pedestal in the middle of the room was a large stone that was surrounded by a bright blue light. Chrane found himself unable to advance any farther as the forces protecting the stone repulsed his presence in the room. His gaze was fixed on this wonder as he savoured its power. Emeralda, on the other hand, moved uninhibited by the forces. She held the tongs out towards the lodestone.

She turned to Chrane. "My lord," she said, interrupting his state of being mesmerized, "you must concentrate and overcome the field surrounding the stone so that I can reach in with my fork and pick the stone off the pedestal. It will be an onerous task but you are so powerful that you will be able to divert the forces and hold them at bay for the short time I need to accomplish my part."

Chrane raised his arm and stared directly ahead at the lodestone. The air was filled with static as he began to chant in an ancient language. Emeralda willed herself not to listen since the chant was hideous to hear and caused extreme revulsion in her mind. Her stomach threatened to spew forth its contents. The air was charged; sparks exploded off the stone walls. Streamers of light flickered and danced all around the pair.

Suddenly, the light around the stone vanished. Emeralda had been anticipating this moment and thrust the fork under the stone. All she had to do was lift it free from the pedestal. She never had the opportunity.

Just as suddenly as the force field had ended, it returned as Chrane let out an agonizing scream. Before Emeralda's eyes the wooden fork burst into flame and began to burn rapidly. She stepped back and released her hold on the tool. It continued to burn quickly.

Emeralda wheeled to face Chrane. She shouted, "You did not hold the force field long enough. I could have had the stone."

Chrane stared at her. "You were too slow! I could not hold it any longer. I gave you the time but you hesitated. Besides, disaster and ruin are upon us. A princess has defeated the dark commander on the field of battle. I have been summoned by my eminence to explain my absence and my failure to maintain the veil of darkness. You have betrayed me. You have over-reached and you have dragged me along with you. You let the fork burn by being too slow in snatching the stone. You failed me when I needed you the most. I will not forget what you tried, so watch your back. If I can, I will be back to make you pay for your treachery."

With a flash, he was gone. Emeralda stared at the spot he had been standing, and then she looked towards the lodestone. The wooden tool continued to burn. She turned and walked out of the room. She stood at the top of the stairs for a moment, looked back longingly for an instant and then walked down the steps away from the castle. She knew she had only a short period of time to get away from the valley before a group of Sages would show up to investigate the fluctuation in the field caused by Chrane's blocking spell. Once she was out of the valley, she could transform into a crow and fly away to an area where she could leave Gorn. Emeralda headed back up the path on which she had so recently arrived. She did not look back.

-26-

Suzy opened her eyes as she heard Timmy calling her. She sat up and looked around to see that the cave was brightly lit. The soldiers had cleaned it up and now the fire was burning brightly. Timmy called to her.

"Come on, Suzy, wake up. See who is here."

Suzy looked in his direction and then she cried out with glee. "Sapphira, you are back." She looked over and spotted Marlen seated by the fire, smiling at her. "Oh, Marlen, isn't this wonderful. Sapphira has returned."

Marlen nodded and stood up. "Come, young princess, I have something to show you." Marlen lead Suzy and Timmy out of the cave where they saw a large army in white assembled. As the two young adventurers stepped into the light, a great cheer went up. Timmy and Suzy waved to the army.

Marlen then spoke, "They are applauding the prince and princess who have driven one facet of darkness out of this land. I went earlier to see the castle in which I was imprisoned and it is now in ruins. All the creatures of this region assembled before it after the dark had fallen and they hammered on its walls until great cracks appeared and then it was rent asunder. Its fall caused the quake that we felt in the cave. The two of you are now legends in Gorn."

Neither of the two children replied because they were overwhelmed with the great celebration. They were led to a pair of ponies, which had been prepared for them to leave. Blog came up to them and handed each a bowl of cooked cereal to serve as their morning meal. After they had consumed the food, they mounted the ponies and followed Marlen and Sapphira who led them away from the place that had once been evil and dark. After a journey back, they celebrated with the white army for a few days and then after many farewells, especially to Blog and his troop who had become very close friends of theirs, Suzy and Timmy accompanied Marlen to the fishing hole where they had a chance to say goodbye to this dear friend.

As Marlen turned to leave, he smiled and said, "Be always ready to spread the good news and good cheer that the two of you possess. We need more of it."

Suzy gave him one last hug, "Oh Marlen, will we ever meet again?"

Marlen gave her a pat on the head and said, "Little princess, we have no idea what is still in store for us. It is quite possible that our paths could again cross and when they do we will again share some time and some adventure."

Then, he was gone.

The children began to walk home. Emeralda, who was standing by the pines, met them.

"So you had to go and release the old fool from his prison. Well, be forewarned, I am not finished with you yet. I know, little Missy, you have my earring but I can not get near the house because there is some force in there that is too strong for me."

Suzy laughed. "That's my mom and her deep love. But you would not understand that, would you?"

"I do know that I want my earring." Emeralda turned, walked away and soon was gone.

Timmy said to Suzy, "She is one to watch out for."

Suzy just shrugged her shoulders and the two children then continued on their way to their own homes.